MY BROTHER,
MY FRIEND . . . MURDERED!

Jordan Maitland was stretched out on his back in the dirt, a dark blotch spreading on the blue-checked shirt, his unbuckled gun belt lying at his side. Rupe fell to his knees beside his brother. Jordan was still breathing, the dark brown eyes opening as Rupe lifted him in his arms.

Jordan looked smaller and younger somehow, and beads of sweat stood out on his face. His lips moved slowly, painfully.

"Early crossed me, Rupe. Damned fool—to let him. Undid my gun belt—he threw down on me . . ."

"I'll get you to the doctor, Jord."

"No use, Rupe. I know—I'm done," Jordan panted. "Tell Dad—it's all right. Tell Karen—nothin'. I was—a fool—Rupe."

A crimson gush drowned his feeble voice and drenched Rupe's sleeve. The bright head dropped back, the eyes open but fixed in a vacant stare at the molten-blue sky. Tenderly, Rupe lowered him to the earth and stood upright, tall and stark.

"So it was murder." He scarcely realized he spoke. He knew what he must do.

THE KANSAN

Roe Richmond

BANTAM BOOKS

TORONTO • NEW YORK • LONDON • SYDNEY • AUCKLAND

THE KANSAN

*A Bantam Book / published by arrangement with
the author's estate*

Bantam edition / October 1987

ISBN 0-553-26811-2

Published simultaneously in the United States and Canada

*Bantam Books are published by Bantam Books, Inc. Its trademark,
consisting of the words "Bantam Books" and the portrayal of a
rooster, is Registered in U.S. Patent and Trademark Office and in
other countries. Marca Registrada. Bantam Books, Inc., 666 Fifth
Avenue, New York, New York 10103.*

THE KANSAN

Chapter 1

Kansas Territory in 1856, torn asunder by murderous warfare between the slavers and the Free Staters, the South and the North. Bleeding Kansas, where the War of the Rebellion really began, long before Harpers Ferry and Fort Sumter and the First Manassas . . .

Rupe Maitland never would forget that great, bearded old man, with the burning eyes, bitter mouth, and the face of a hawk. John Brown, nearly sixty, with seven big sons towering at his broad back. Old Brown of Osawatomie, they called him, with two revolving pistols and a bowie knife sagging his belt, a blood-encrusted saber in his huge, veined hand.

"How do you stand on that goose?" he asked, the same question that had been hurled at the Browns when they arrived fresh out of Ohio, living in tents while they cleared the land in Kansas.

"Why, we try to be neutral," Rupe's father said.

Those fierce eyes flamed through them. "Neutral?" John Brown said, as if it were a strange new word. "You don't look like cowards. Neither you nor your two boys."

"We aren't," Frank Maitland said simply.

"You hold with slavery?"

"No, we don't believe in slavery. We'd never own slaves ourselves. But if other men want to, isn't that their right? We don't consider it our cause."

"It's the cause of every human being alive in the world today!" thundered John Brown, touching the Bible in his

1

frayed pocket with a gnarled hand. "Slavery's against the Book and against God!"

Frank Maitland was silent, standing like a rock between his two sons, Rupert and Jordan, who were trying not to show their fear. These Browns were killers, almost as bad as Atchinson's Assassins on the proslavery side. Near the Marais de Cygnes, the Browns had routed five slavers out of bed in the middle of the night, killing them with sabers to keep it quiet, while John Brown said, "Right is everything."

"Nobody is neutral in Kansas!" said Old John Brown. "Nobody can live in Kansas and remain on the fence. You think it over, Maitland, you and your boys here. We'll be back, when God grants us time."

The Browns were gone now, eastward somewhere along the dark, tortuous and doomed road, the fanatical way that led to Harpers Ferry, death for sons and disciples, and the gallows at Charlestown for Old John Brown.

But war still raged in Kansas, rending the Territory with strife and gunblasts and flaming torches, and no settler's life was safe. Men were shot down over their ploughs, or as they came with slopping milkpails from the barnyard chores. Shot from their saddles or wagon seats on the way to market in town. Killed in barroom brawls and back-alley fights. Shot through lamplit windows at night, or on dewy doorsteps as they emerged at sunrise . . . The worst kind of warfare.

Morning sunlight filled the kitchen, where the breakfast fragrance of ham and eggs, toast and coffee, still lingered. A masculine household since Mom had died and Melora had married. The chores were done, but dirty dishes were still stacked on the sinkboard. No matter how friendly and pleasant a house was, it seemed empty, barren and incomplete without the presence and touch of a woman. Rupert Maitland was aware of this as he scraped the razor along his hard jawbones, cleansing the bronzed skin of lather and coppery beard stubble.

The face reflected in the mirror was angular and strong-boned, with clear gray eyes that were level, steady and intensely keen. The short-cut hair tousled above the high broad forehead was a tawny sun-streaked blond on a well-shaped skull. The nose proud and sharp and slightly tilted, the mouth wide and handsomely curved, sensitive and mobile yet firm. The chin clear-cut and faintly cleft, flaring into the clean bleak lines of the jaws. A face that could be savage in anger, charming when creased by the easy boyish smile: rough-hewn and homely, but pleasant and somehow striking. Rupert grimaced at it as he razored the last of the suds and bristles.

"Hurry up, Rupe," said Jordan Maitland, slamming through the screen door into the room and grinning at his elder brother.

"Karen will keep, Jord," said Rupert, bending over the washbasin and sloshing water lavishly.

"I don't know, Rupe, with all those Southern cavaliers around."

"They never bothered me much."

"Maybe they were afraid of you, but not of your kid brother."

Toweling his face and head, Rupert smiled soberly at Jordan. Thus far the bitter dissension had not touched the Maitlands directly. In spite of John Brown's warning, they had maintained a strict, if precarious, neutrality. Frank Maitland was a strong, independent man, a quietly resolute individual, and his sons had the same qualities, sharpened with youthful will and pride. They were a New England family, close-knit, integrated, somewhat withdrawn and aloof. The Maitlands minded their own business, respected the privacy of others, and expected their fellowmen to do likewise.

Lounging on a table, Jordan shaped and lighted a cigarette. He was already scrubbed and clean-shaven, his bright brown curls glistening wet but unruly in spite of brush and comb, his dark brown eyes lighted happily as he whistled a gay tune. Not quite as tall as Rupe, Jordan was built broad and solid like his father, with finely carved features and an easy, winning manner. He wore a clean, gray flannel shirt checked with blue, his best blue trousers and polished boots, a new light gray hat set back on his head, and a gun belt with the holstered Remington .44. A handsome, carefree young man, for all of the hardships, tragedies and turbulent troubled times on the frontier.

Frank Maitland entered quickly, smoking a pipe and smiling gravely at his two tall sons. "Another Saturday. Sometimes I wish I was a little younger."

"Why don't you ride in with Jord, Dad?" asked Rupert. "I've got nothin' special to go for."

"Neither have I, Rupe," said Frank. "Melora and Nick'll be out tomorrow. I'd rather putter around here than go into town." He smiled his slow, grave smile. "Sign of advancin' age, I guess."

Frank Maitland had aged since his wife's death, but at fifty he was still young and active. A patient, thoughtful man, kind, gentle and tolerant—a gracious man of broad sympathy and understanding, with a quiet, willful strength under his serene calm. Never goaded by greed or scourged by ambition, Frank Maitland had lived a good, full life in a simple, modest way. He was still fine-looking; wide and stalwart with thinning brown hair, straight features, mild brown eyes, and a broad mouth that was both generous and firm.

"All right, Dad," said Rupert. "I'll try to keep the kid here out of trouble."

Rupert was taller and rangier than the other two, with a sloping breadth of shoulder and tremendous long arms and legs, built spare and lean, like a greyhound of exceptional power and rugged stamina. He shrugged into a fresh sun-faded blue shirt and tucked it into his worn pants, not troubling to dress up for the trip to town. Lifting his filled shell belt off its peg, he buckled it on and thonged the holstered .44 Walker Colt to his right thigh. Pulling on a leather vest with its handy pockets, and a flat-crowned wide-brimmed black hat, Rupert was ready to travel.

"The team's harnessed up, I hope," he drawled.

"Sure, that's what you've been stallin' around for," laughed Jordan.

"You've got the list, Rupe," said Frank. "Don't forget to bring a couple of jugs, now."

Jordan grinned. "Don't worry, Dad. That's one thing Rupe'll never forget."

"Sure, I'll take the whiskey," Rupert said. "You take the girls, Jord. And you'll get in trouble way ahead of me, boy. And way more serious."

"I don't know," protested Jordan. "That was quite a ruckus you had with Elwood Kivett and Huber Northrup."

"Good, clean fun. Nobody killed, nobody hurt—much."

"Stay away from those slavers," advised Frank. "They're always forcin' a fight and then gangin' up on somebody. I'm sorry to hear young Early Hessler's in with that bunch now."

"I'm goin' to have to muss that boy up myself," Jordan said. "Even if he is Karen's big brother. Early's got a nasty tongue in his head at times. Worse since he's been runnin' with Kivett, Northrup, Sporn and Tattam—that crowd of Chance Charrick's."

"They figure they're pretty tough," Rupert said. "They've shot a few Free State farmers in the back and they fancy themselves as real killers."

"A strange thing," mused Frank Maitland, "that people of the same blood and color and country can't live together in peace."

After the boys had driven away in the spring sunshine, rattling and bumping in the flat-bed wagon behind the matched buckskins, Frank Maitland refilled and lighted his stubby pipe and went to washing the dishes. His wife Milly had died in the freezing cold of last winter, and Melora, the youngest child, had married Nick Santell and gone to live in the nearby town of Trayborough, a trading center in the Osawatomie region in Kansas. Nick Santell was a staunch Abolitionist, and the community was populated with sympathizers to both causes. Jordan was courting Karen Hessler, whose father Clay and brother Early were among the Southern pro-slavery leaders in Trayborough. Everything was all mixed up, Frank thought, but one thing was dead certain: the homestead was a lonely place with both women gone.

The dishes done, Frank walked slowly to his wife's

grave on the cedar-shaded knoll behind the house and sat down in the tender new grass by the headstone. As much as he loved his sons, Frank looked forward to these Saturdays when he was left alone with Millicent. It seemed then that they were close together again. With the boys around, Frank stayed away from the grave, but when they were gone, he felt free to talk to his dead wife. It seemed fitting only when he was alone on the farm.

The world had a rain-washed freshness this morning, the grass sprouting bright green and the trees shimmering with delicate amber-green young leaves. The creek glittered through the feathery lance-leafed boughs of the cottonwoods and silver-tipped willows. The buildings below looked clean and neat, snug and secure, but it wasn't the same place with Millicent missing, and Melora. The vast sweeping plains of Kansas rolled away, endless as a bronze ocean, to the far hazed horizons, but it was an empty, barren land without Milly.

"Summer's comin' again, Milly," he said softly. "If you could only have waited, if you could've stayed till spring, you'd be well now. It's hard and lonesome without you, but I shouldn't be complainin'. We had a good life together, while it lasted. The boys are fine, Milly, and Melora's marriage is turnin' out well. Nick Santell's a good man, I think, although maybe a little hotheaded on the slave question. We aren't mixed up in that yet, but I'm afraid we will be sooner or later. I'm afraid Old Brown was right: 'Nobody's neutral in Kansas.'"

A breeze sprang up, riffling the cedars, and the grass whispered green-gold in the sunlight, as if Millicent were answering in a sweet, low breath from somewhere. Frank shivered slightly as that rustling sound went through him. . . . Balmy winds blowing up from Mexico way, mellowing the bite of the breeze from the Dakotas, and the stunted peach trees were blossoming pink and white along the stone wall.

"The corn's startin' up early and the wheat's prickin' through, Milly," went on Frank Maitland. "It'll be a good year if the chintz locusts stay out of the sorghum and the insect plagues pass us by and it rains enough to keep off another drought. The cattle and horses wintered all right, the hogs are fattenin', the hens layin' well. . . ."

His voice caught in his throat and trailed off into the rippling grass. *But it's aching-empty with you gone, Milly. The warmth out of the sun, the brightness out of the sky, the magic gone from things growin' in the earth. Sunrise and sunset colors dimmed, the dream broken, the music faded, the wonder dissolved. The blood slow and thin, the flesh weary and the bones tired and brittle, the beauty vanished forever. Without you.*

"We're gettin' along fine and dandy," Frank Maitland's low voice came again. "No call for you to worry and fret over us. But we sure miss you, Milly, we all miss you. And it's not the same without you; it never can be the same, my dear."

Chapter 2

Jouncing along the western road to Trayborough, Rupert
relaxed in the warmth of the soaring sun at their backs,
while Jordan handled the reins, too brimming with restless
life and vitality to sit idly on the wagon seat. Dust swirled
up from the hoofs of the buckskins, pungent and pleasant
on the golden air, and insects hummed about horses and
men. At twenty-seven, two years older than Jord, Rupert
still felt that Jordan was a kid brother to be watched over
and protected. Ridiculous in a way, for Jord was fully as
heavy and even stronger than Rupe, but the feeling
persisted. From boyhood days in Vermont, Rupe had been
his brother's guide and guardian.

They were friends as well as brothers, and they
enjoyed being together more than most brothers do. More
than friends because they were brothers, and closer than
brothers because they were friends. While the wagon
rumbled along in the sunshot dust, they talked casually—
about the farm, which sometimes bored and always held
them. Dad, whom they frankly worshiped. Melora and her
husband, Nick Santell, whom they liked, even though he
had taken their sister away. Karen Hessler, who had been
Rupe's girl before she was Jordan's. Chance Carrick's crew
of Southerners, whom they detested, and half-mad
Preacher Pratt, the most bloodthirsty and murderous of all
Atchinson's slavers. And the Abolitionist party led by Reef
Bassett and Henry Holdcroft, toward which they leaned.
Their mother wasn't mentioned, but she was always in their
minds wherever they went.

They argued a bit about slavery. "It's wrong for men to *own* other men, no matter what their color is," Jordan insisted. "To buy and sell and punish them like animals."

"Of course it's wrong," admitted Rupert. "But I still say it's a matter of climate and geography. If the North was a hot, cotton- and tobacco-raisin' country, they'd want slaves as much as the South."

"Maybe so. But that don't make it any more right."

"No. But it makes you wonder why Northerners are so bitter against slavery," Rupert said, in his slow, soft voice. "I feel like Dad. Let them live their way and we'll live ours."

"But slavery's an evil thing. It ought to be wiped out, Rupe."

Rupert smiled. "There are lots of evil things that ought to be wiped out, Jord."

"I can't argue with you, Rupe," complained Jordan, scowling. "You agree and still disagree. But you can't deny slavery is rotten. You've got to admit the Negroes should be freed."

"How do you know they *want* to be freed?"

Jordan snorted. "Who wouldn't want to? We've seen enough runaway slaves come north. Heard enough about how they're whipped and beaten, branded, tortured and killed."

"You can't believe all those stories, Jord. And when you consider all the slaves in the South, there aren't so many runnin' away."

"What about the way they treat the colored women? You've heard Early Hessler and Kivett, Northrup, Sporn and Tattam brag about their wenches."

"Compared to some of the field hands, they have a fairly easy time," Rupert drawled.

Jordan swore in exasperation. "Hell, you don't like it any better than I do. You just want to argue around it, Rupe."

"It's only fair to see both sides, son," Rupert said, smiling. "But of course you're young and headstrong and know-it-all."

Jordan spat disgustedly over the wheel. "And you're so

damn old and wise! Tell you one thing, Rupe: Havin' slaves
makes people feel like gods. Look at Early and the rest of
them young Southerners. High-headed and uppity as wild
stallions."

"What about Karen?"

"She's not that way, and you know it," Jordan declared.
"Someday I'm goin' to take that Early apart, though. I like
him, too, but he gets damn aggravatin' at times."

The eastern outskirts of Trayborough were dominated
by the large brown and gray fieldstone mansion of the
Hesslers, with its white-pillared façade in the Southern
tradition. Honeysuckle clustered the white picket fence
bordering the expansive grounds, and Cherokee roses
brightened the velvet lawn. Magnolias were in bloom with
large fragrant blossoms of pink, white and purple. By far
the grandest place in the area, it looked pretentious and out
of place in this raw, crude frontier settlement of frame, log
and even sod houses. Rupert Maitland regarded it with the
same resentment and distaste that he had come to feel for
Karen Hessler. Too rich and showy, perfumed and polished,
elegant and superior. People like the Hesslers should have
stayed in the South.

Clay Hessler, with plenty of money to invest, was said
to be the silent partner behind most of the stores, saloons
and business enterprises of Trayborough, and held mort-
gages on many outlying farms and ranches. A tall, refined,
darkly handsome man, he was president of the Trayborough
Trust and Savings Bank, as well as a renowned horseman,
pistol shot and swordsman. It was rumored that a duel,
ending fatally for Clay Hessler's opponent, had led to his
leaving Georgia and coming West.

Early, Clay's son, was supposed to be reading law with
Judge Moultrie, but spent most of his time riding or
swaggering about with Chance Carrick's Slave Staters.

Jordan pulled up at the roadside before Hessler Hall,
frowning when he saw three young men on the porch with
Karen, quickly identifying them with narrowed brown eyes
and tautened lips. Big Shaw Tattam, black and brawny in
one of his checkered shirts, surly and sullen, with a growing

reputation as a fist- and gunfighter. Stocky, broad-faced
Huber Northrup, well-tailored and serenely sure of himself, extravagantly gallant in manner. And Elwood Kivett,
slender and graceful, dashing and debonair, dressing like a
dandified fop, but nonetheless dangerous.

Shaw Tattam glowered at the wagon, while Huber
Northrup raised his tall glass in a half-mocking salute.
Elwood Kivett called out in a clear, gay voice: "The trade
entrance is around to the rear, my good men!" Then,
laughing: "How are you, Jord? Join us for a drink?" Almost
everyone liked Jordan, whereas Rupert was either liked or
disliked intensely.

"Are you stoppin', Jord?" inquired Rupert, taking this
opportunity to roll and light a cigarette.

Jordan thought briefly. "No, to hell with it. Not with
them there." He slapped the reins and spoke to the horses,
but Karen Hessler left the veranda and ran lightly down the
long flagstone walk as the wagon started moving again.
Jordan reined up, muttering to himself, and Rupert
grinned at him. "Looks like you're still Number One, kid."

"Yeah? Half the time I have the feelin' that she'd rather
have you back," grumbled Jordan.

"Wrong there," murmured Rupert. "But she does have
trouble makin' up that butterfly mind of hers. Want me to
wait?"

"No, I'll walk downtown in a few minutes." Jordan
handed him the reins and swung lithely to the ground.

"Don't tangle with all three of them, Jord," warned
Rupert, watching his brother stride across the sunny road.

The odor of honeysuckle and magnolia came to him
with a pang, and Rupe remembered the bright days and
moonlit evenings he had spent here with the slim, vivid girl
who was coming to meet Jordan. It still hurt, still left an
emptiness and loneliness, but Rupert felt that his judgment
had been correct. Karen was too volatile and elusive, too
high-faluting and flirty. A man could break his heart trying
to reach and know and hold her. Karen was a lovely will-o'-
the-wisp, without substance, meaning or depth.

He clucked at the buckskins with a slap of the reins

and drove on, unaware that Karen's dark gaze flickered over Jord's broad shoulders and followed his back down the sunlit road. The South was full of slick, winsome girls like her, Rupert supposed. Pampered, petted, spoiled creatures, smiling behind fans or across candlelit tables, dancing in great brilliant ballrooms, reigning over retinues of lovesick young swains, flirting with one beau after another. Trained coquettes and spectral beauties, accepting everything as their just due, giving nothing in return, nothing of themselves beyond a teasing smile, a delicate hand to kiss. Well, that was not for Rupe Maitland. He preferred a lively, laughing, full-bodied girl like Dodie Deneen, the copper-haired queen of the Redwing dance hall.

Leaning over the gate, Karen Hessler was laughing up at Jordan Maitland with roguish dark eyes, set at a slight exotic tilt and crinkled charmingly at the corners, her full-curved red lips parted on her perfect white teeth. Karen's black hair had a burnished sheen in the sunlight, waving naturally back from the wide pure brow. Her features were finely sculptured, a blend of delicacy and strength, the cheeks highboned and the jaws firm and clear-cut, the line from lifted chin to throat classic and lovely. Her lissome body had a lush feminine depth at breast and hip, fashioned in full flowing curves, flawlessly filling the trim gray blouse and flared blue skirt.

"Come on up to the house, Jord," she invited. "I know you'd like a drink after that hot, dusty ride."

"Haven't got time, Karen. Got to help Rupe in town."

"Holding up Gunnarsson's bar, you mean? Rupe can take care of that by himself. You aren't angry because the boys are here, Jord? It's the free liquor that draws them more than myself. You know they don't mean anything to me, darling."

"Yeah, I know."

"They're amusing, of course. At least Elwood and Huber are. That Shaw Tattam gives me the shivers sometimes. But you're the only one I want to be with."

"I'll see you tonight, Karen," said Jordan, hoarse with his need for this sleek, scented girl, his big hands white-knuckled on the gate.

"And waste this whole beautiful afternoon?" she protested.

"It won't be wasted. You have company enough."

"They're riding out soon, Jord. They aren't staying long."

"Going out to bushwhack some Free Staters?" Jordan inquired, with malice.

Karen frowned petulantly. "I don't know or care where they're going or what they're going to do. I gather that you don't approve of Early's friends?"

"I don't approve of anybody who kills from ambush."

"Have you any proof that they do, Jordan?" asked Karen coldly.

"No, but some of them brag about it when they're drunk. Everybody knows who's killin' the Abolitionists around here."

"Well, let's not quarrel about it." She leaned across the gate, lifting her mouth to him, and Jordan kissed her quickly, not caring for an audience. A faint mock cheer went up from the colonnaded porch, and Jordan's jaws squared and hardened with muscle. "Stop off on your way back then, Jord," said Karen.

Jordan nodded his brown head. "I will, Karen—if you're alone."

"I'll be alone, darling," she promised, and watched him walk away in the direction of town, a fine, handsome figure of a man, with an easy-swinging stride, a slight unconscious swagger. Better looking by far than his brother, yet there was something about Rupert that a girl couldn't forget, try as she might. . . .

Back on the veranda, Huber Northrup remarked on Karen's return, "There's no accounting for taste, and that's an unfortunate fact. This wayward girl could have exclusively my charming and cultured company, yet she dawdles away her time on that big dirt farmer."

"Perhaps Jord appeals to the primitive in her," Elwood

Kivett said. "Gentlemen like ourselves are too mild and decadent. There's a lot of the savage and elemental in all women, you know."

Shaw Tattam, reaching a huge hand out for the cut-glass decanter, scowlingly refilled his glass, and said nothing.

Chapter 3

Driving on toward Trayborough's business section, Rupert Maitland passed through the eastern residential district, which had a few fieldstone and frame houses scattered among the plank shacks, log cabins and sod-roofed huts. Children played in the yards, dogs ran barking after horsemen and vehicles, and the holiday atmosphere of Saturday prevailed in general. Front Street, which had been a wallow of mud in the rainy season, was now fetlock-deep in dust. Nearer the center, there were false-fronted stores with overhanging wooden awnings, their porches piled with crates and bales, boxes and barrels. The hitch rails here were lined with saddle horses, buggies, buck-boards, and wagons of every variety. Most of the men along the boardwalks wore belted guns, and many of them also carried rifles. A frontier settlement without any alleviating grace, there was a primitive, lawless aspect about Trayborough.

An open square, surrounded by business places with a large stone watering trough at the center, formed the nucleus of the community. Here were the principal markets and stores and the Jayhawker Hotel, the two-story brick bank building, and the long low stone structure of Gunnarsson's Saloon. West of the central plaza, Front Street was flanked mainly by the Redwing dance hall, saloons, gambling houses, cafés, poolrooms, and out in the squalid fringes, the all-night dives and honky-tonks.

Rupert found an opening for the buckskins and wagon, had a drink in Gunnarsson's, and went about buying the necessary provisions and supplies, exchanging greetings with friends and acquaintances here and there. Jord was seldom of much assistance on these shopping trips, and today the fact irritated Rupe more than usual. He didn't like Jord's attachment to Karen in the first place, and he begrudged the time he might otherwise have spent with Dodie Deneen.

The air was charged with tension these days, an ominous feeling that trouble and strife might break out at any minute. Southern slavers and Northern Free Staters eyed one another with wary suspicion and open hatred. Recently there had been frequent fistfights, rough-and-tumble gang brawls, and occasional shooting scrapes that ended in bloodshed and death. It was always self-defense in these cases, especially when the slavers had the better of it, and the law did little or nothing about them. People said that Clay Hessler kept Judge Moultrie and Marshal Leck-onby in his vest pocket.

In the grain and feed mill on his last errand, Rupert was impatient to get away, but Brownlee, the miller, felt like talking: "They say Chance Carrick and them hellers of his are in town, liquored up and rarin' to go. There's been some talk of 'em hittin' your place, Rupe. Don't want to upset you none, and it's probably nothin' but gossip, but I thought you ought to know. Frank Maitland is thought a lot of in these parts, and you boys, too."

"Thanks anyway, Browny," said Rupert. "I don't see why they'd be hittin' us, but I guess they might do most anythin'."

Brownlee nodded morbidly. "Yeah, they're like a pack of mad dogs or starved-out wolves. Decent folks ain't safe in their own homes no more. The Osawatomie ain't a fit place to live with them hellhounds of Carrick's runnin' wild."

Rupert was dragging hundred-pound grain sacks toward the door when Jordan came in with a sheepish grin. "Just in time as usual, huh, Rupe?"

"You're a big help," agreed Rupert, dropping one sack for his brother and hauling the other out onto the loading platform. Jordan had just heaved his bag into the wagon bed when Early Hessler crossed the yard and sprang up beside them.

"Well, well, how are the Yankee brothers today?" he inquired jovially, clapping Jord on the back and smiling coolly at Rupe.

"Good enough," Jordan said. "How's the flower of Southern aristocracy?"

"Right in the prime," laughed Hessler. "A few more drinks'll put me in full bloom, Jord."

Early Hessler was taller by an inch than Jord, almost up to Rupe's six-two height, dark and handsome like his father, with flashing, scornful black eyes and a superior smile. Powerfully built and graceful in his expensively tailored suit, with an arrogant pride in his chiseled features, the tilt of his glossy dark head, and his swashbuckling manner. He stood now with varnished boots apart and thumbs in gun belt, insolently sure of himself with the matched bone-handled Colts sheathed on his thighs. A rakish figure, always posing and play-acting a little, boastful of his drinking and gambling, riding, fighting.

"Come on, Jordy, I'll buy the drinks," Early Hessler said. "Big brother can attend to the rest of this dull business."

"Sure, go ahead, Jord," said Rupert. "I'll meet you in Gunnarsson's in a little while."

They walked away laughing merrily together, Hessler's arm draped about Jordan's wide shoulders. Rupert watched them out of sight, vaguely disturbed. There was something about Early Hessler that Rupe didn't like, never had liked, even when he'd been deeply infatuated with Karen. From the beginning, Rupert had felt that sometime, somewhere, he would face Early Hessler in a fight to the death. Several times they had been on the brink of battle, but something always had intervened to break it up before a blow was struck or a draw started. But it would come someday.

Stepping to the wagon seat, Rupert unwrapped the reins and swung the loaded wagon around into a shady spot out of the way of traffic. Now he was free to seek a little relaxation of his own. Walking to the rear of the Redwing, he saw Dodie Deneen watching from her second-floor window and saluted in response to her smile and wave. Dirty-faced urchins hooted at him as he climbed the gritty creaking outside stairway at the back of the building, and Dodie had the door unlocked and open for him.

In the fragrant haven of her room, Dodie bolted the door with a sigh of satisfaction and turned eagerly to him. "Ah, Rupe, it's a long time between Saturdays."

"A long time for me, chasin' cows and mendin' fence and grubbin' in the field," Rupe Maitland said. "But it ought to go fast in a busy place like this, Dodie."

"It don't," she said, moving close and locking her arms strongly about him, pressing herself hard against his rangy frame, raising her ripe mouth with frank, honest hunger. Rupe held her close, crushing the sweet fullness of her lips under his, breathing in the perfume of her coppery red hair. A woman like this was what a man needed, warm, living flesh and blood. No teasing or hand-kissing, no false shyness or gentility. A girl like Dodie made a man feel good, bursting with life and power, just the way she looked up at him with genuine appreciation and understanding. Her embrace made him wholly alive and happy.

Dodie Deneen freed herself with a breathless laugh. "Ah, but that's good, Rupe! Better all the time. Wait a minute and I'll get us a drink." She moved away with lazy swaying grace, the supple rounded lines of her body flowing with infinite ease. High-breasted, willowy in the waist, superbly hipped, she had a figure that took a man's breath away. The luxuriant red hair was natural, untouched, agleam from brushing, and her face was keen, sharp-featured and striking, only a trifle hardened, a shade weary.

Rupe smiled as he accepted the glass, clinked it to hers.

They toasted one another in silent fondness. Dodie was a woman hundreds of men had courted, he knew, but few had piqued her interest, and none since she'd met Rupert. He made no claim on her; it was Dodie's own decision, and she asked nothing of him in return. "Entertaining 'em in the dance parlor's my business," she had said, "but that's all they are to me. I don't expect you to marry me or anythin'. It's just the way I want it, that's all. One day a week, at least, I'll live!"

Rupe had just drained his glass when a commotion broke out in the nearby square, and something clutched at his throat as he went to the window. Below, he saw an excited crowd surging and milling around in front of Gunnarsson's, growing constantly as men ran in from all directions. Apparently a fight had started, and Rupe thought instantly of Jordan, a cold premonition chilling his mind, a hollow flutter of panic in his chest.

"What is it, Rupe?" asked Dodie.

"Some kind of trouble," Rupe said, grabbing his hat and gun belt. "Jord's down there, Dodie. I've got to go."

Dodie threw herself upon him as Rupe strapped on the belt. "No, Rupe! You can't leave me. Jord's big enough to look out for himself. What difference'll one more man make in that mob?"

"Don't try to stop me." Rupe shucked the heavy gun into place on his right thigh, and unwound the girl's clinging arms, pushing her away with gentle firmness.

"Please, Rupe! This is our day. We only have one a week. You can't go!" She flung herself at him again, fierce and possessive as never before.

Rupe Maitland thrust her roughly aside, his gray eyes flaring, cheekbones and jaws standing out until they stretched the bronze skin, his mouth a broad straight line. "Damn it, he's my brother, Dodie!" Driving past her, Rupe strode out of the room, through the outside door, and stomped down the backstairs. Once on the ground he started running toward the square, holding down on the Colt as he ran, fear like a sinking sickness in the pit of his stomach.

Long springing strides carried him swiftly past other running men to the outer ranks of the jostling throng. A gun cracked as he plunged into the heaving mass of humanity, and a long-drawn gasp went through the crowd. Tall as he was, Rupe couldn't see what was happening ahead, but he made out several men breaking from the center and fleeing for Gunnarsson's.

Indignant faces turned on Rupert as he fought his way

through the close-packed bodies, using his elbows and shoulders, knees and hips. He noticed none of them, felt none of the jarring contacts, until a slaver named Breen whirled and sledged a heavy fist at him. Pulling away and pivoting back in, Rupe poured everything into a lashing left hand that caught Breen squarely in the bearded face, jerking the shag-head back and dropping him out of sight among the massed writhing men. *Take that, you sonofabitch!*

Rupe went on with driving legs and flogging shoulders, and when he neared the inner circle resentment faded from the blurred bobbing faces and men made way for him. He knew then that Jordan was involved—hurt, dying or dead in there. Fury filled him, and Rupe burst into the central ring like a madman.

Jordan was stretched out on his back in the dirt, a dark blotch spreading on the blue-checked gray shirt, his unbuckled gun belt lying loosely at his side. Rupe fell to his knees beside his brother. Jordan was still breathing, still alive, the dark brown eyes opening as Rupe lifted him into his arms. The bright brown curls were dust-smeared, and enormous beads of sweat stood out on Jord's face. He looked smaller and younger somehow, heartbreakingly young under the tan and streaks of dirt. His lips moved slowly, painfully, and Rupe saw death in Jordan's face.

"Crossed me, Rupe—Early did. Damn fool—to let him. Undid my belt—and he drew." Jordan wagged his head in wry disgust.

"I'll get you to the doctor, Jord."

"No use, Rupe. I know—I'm done," Jordan panted. "Tell Dad—it's all right. Tell Karen—nothin'. I was—a fool—Rupe."

A crimson gush drowned his feeble voice and drenched Rupe's sleeve. The bright head drooped back, the brown eyes still open but fixed in a vacant stare at the molten-blue sky. Tenderly, Rupe lowered him to the earth and stood upright, tall and stark.

"So, it was murder." He scarcely realized that he spoke.

A confused babble arose: "Murder, all right . . ." "I

wouldn't say so . . ." "Who in hell asked you?" "It was to
be bare knuckles, goddammit!" "Jord was unhookin' his belt
when Early plugged him . . ." "You can't trust a slaver
scum . . ." "Watch your filthy tongue, mister!"

"Where's Hessler?" asked Rupe dully.

"Dusted off, Rupe," said someone. "Him and Chance
Carrick and the whole bunch. Kivett and Asa Sporn,
Northrup, Tattam—all of 'em. Lined out with drawn guns."

"He's started runnin'," Rupe Maitland murmured, as if
to himself. "He'll be runnin' now until he's dead." He
thought bitterly, *If I hadn't gone to Dodie . . . If I'd
stayed with Jord, he'd be alive and all right. But I had to
see her, so Jord is dead. Jesus Christ, Jord, my brother, my
friend.*

Rupert saw men stooping to raise another crumpled
figure from the dust. He recognized Nick Santell's ruffled
auburn crest, with blood trickling down his forehead from
the reddish hair, and looked into Nick's blue eyes, stricken
but blazing with anger and hatred. Freeing himself from
the supporting arms, Santell staggered toward Rupe,
spitting dirt and shaking his head. Not a large man, Nick
Santell was wiry and tough as rawhide, quick with his hands
and a gun.

"I saw what was goin' to happen, Rupe," he said
glumly. "I was reachin' when some sonofabitch belted me
over the head with a gun barrel."

"Elwood Kivett." A bystander supplied the name. "I
saw him club you down, Nick."

"It don't matter much," Nick Santell said. "They're all
goin' to die for this. Every slavin' one of 'em!"

"What happened, Nick?" asked Rupert.

"They was drinkin' together in Gunnarsson's and
arguin' a little, good-natured at first. Then Early Hessler
said somethin' about no damn dirt-grubbin' Yankee was
good enough for his sister, and it flared up real sudden.
They moved outside to fight barehanded. Jord unbuckled
his gun belt, and Early drew and shot him. I was down
myself by that time, but I saw the start of it and heard the
shot, and I knew how it was. Plain murder, Rupe. Jord
never had a chance."

"I knew it when I saw his belt off," Rupert said. "Help me lug him to the wagon, Nick."

Carrying Jord between them, they started across the square in the glaring sunshine, stopping to rest and get a drink at the stone watering trough in the center. The crowd had dispersed and drifted away for the most part, but many people were watching them from awning-shaded sidewalks, doors and windows about the plaza. Rupert wet a clean handkerchief and bathed Jord's face while Nick Santell ducked his own aching head into the water. Then they went on to the feedstore yard and laid Jordan's body carefully in the wagon bed. Rupe covered it with a horse blanket, leaving the shell belt and Remington .44 beside Jord. Brownlee stood on the loading platform, shaking his bowed graying head and mumbling miserably to himself.

"You got everythin' bought, Rupe?" asked Nick Santell. "Well, then, I'll ride along out with you."

"What about Melora, Nick?"

"She'll come out with the Lamberts as soon as they hear about it. Come on, Rupe, let's get out of here."

Nick Santell took the reins, and Rupe Maitland climbed stiffly aboard and sank down beside him on the worn wooden seat, moving mechanically and oblivious to everything around them. He was aware only of one dinning, incredible thought, hammering over and over in his numb brain: *Jord's dead, my brother's dead, Jordan's gone.* It tolled on and on without cease, and still was impossible and meaningless. Rupe could not believe it; it couldn't be true.

Chapter 4

Nick Santell put the team into the square and headed east. People peered furtively as they passed, but Rupe Maitland was only dimly aware of these onlookers and the surroundings. Dodie Deneen had come out of the Redwing to stand on the corner and watch them drive away. O God, he'll blame me, she thought. Rupe'll blame me and never come back. Her green eyes filmed with tears, Dodie turned back toward the dance hall. A man spoke pleasantly to her, then shrank abruptly from the look in her eyes and face.

"This'll really open the ball," somebody predicted gloomily. "Hell's goin' to bust loose in the Osawatomie. From here on a man's life ain't goin' to be worth a plugged penny."

In the creaking wagon, Rupert felt as if he were encased in ice, numbed to the bone, unfeeling and unbelieving, shocked beyond comprehension. Nick reined up in front of Bournot's barroom: "Just be a minute, Rupe."

A curious crowd gathered to stare at the blanket-covered form in the back of the wagon, scattering at once when Rupe turned on the seat to look at them with naked menace. He loathed everyone left alive, and would have killed instantly any man who spoke out of turn or glanced at him the wrong way.

Nick came back with two quart bottles of whiskey, and Rupe said, "We've got a couple jugs in back, Nick."

"It won't go to waste, Rupe," promised Nick Santell. "You can't ever have too much of this stuff, boy." He clucked

23

the horses into motion and uncorked one of the bottles between his knees, handing it to Rupert.

It didn't even burn today; it went down like colored water. Rupe tipped the bottle again, and this time it took hold a little. He felt warmth spreading through the inner numbness, stirring his blood and quickening his pulse. As the numbness wore off, a dry racking grief screamed silently through him, rending and tearing him inside.

"He's dead," Rupe murmured, low and wondering. "Jord's dead. And it was my fault, Nick."

"You're crazy, Rupe. You couldn't watch him every second. And Jord would've been all right if Early hadn't cheated and crossed him."

"I was with Dodie."

"Why the hell not?" Nick Santell said. "You've got a life of your own to live, Rupe."

"To one purpose now—to kill Early Hessler."

Nick drank from the bottle and passed it back. "You'll get him, Rupe. We'll get all of them struttin' back-shooters!"

The whitewashed picket fence and sloping green lawns of Hessler Hall were just ahead of them, and Rupert said, "I'm stoppin' here, Nick. I won't be long."

"What for, Rupe? You'd better not. They might be holed up there."

"No, they rode out of town, I think. I just want to tell her—"

"What if they are waitin' here?"

Rupert smiled bleakly. "Save me a lot of chasin', Nick."

"You can't fight them all."

"I'll take Early. That's all I care about."

Nick shrugged, sighed, and pulled up before the gate. "No horses in the yard. Maybe it's safe enough, Rupe, but make it quick as you can."

Mounting the flagstone walk, Rupe Maitland heard his own tread as if from a distance, the mingled odors of magnolia, honeysuckle and Cherokee roses sickeningly sweet in his senses. The white-columned porch was empty, the great house proud and still in the sunlight. The showplace of the Osawatomie, and how many Negroes did they keep here? Rupe thought, *I ought to start freeing them right here and now. Jord wanted them freed, didn't he?* He yanked the bellpull, and listened to the muted chimes echoing within the mansion.

Karen herself came to the door, her surprise changing to dread and horror as she scanned Rupe's grim, strong-boned face. "Why, Rupe, what in the world—? What's happened, Rupe, to bring you here?"

"Early just killed my brother Jord," said Rupert. "You can tell Early that I'm goin' to kill him on sight."

"Oh, no! My God, *no!*" Karen Hessler's slim hands clutched her face, her dark head sagging as if under a blow. "Rupe, Rupe, it *can't* be so!"

"Would I be lyin' about it?" Rupert wheeled and strode away, deaf to the pleading call she sobbed out, snorting against the Southern perfumes that assailed his nostrils. "I don't know what I did that for," he mused, "unless I wanted her to suffer some, too."

Nick handed him the bottle as he sat down, and Rupe took a long pull at it as the wagon rumbled onward.

The sun soared high in the brassy blue sky and its glare beat down upon them. Dust rose from the plodding hoofs and drifted back to their faces, smelling to Rupe of summer dirt roads in Vermont when he and Jord were barefooted kids. Behind the clopping hoofs the wheels rattled, the axles groaned, and the wagon creaked and rumbled. This rocky, rutted road was strange and foreign to Rupe, as if he hadn't traveled it for years. The whole countryside looked different, weird and distorted in the shimmering heat.

They drank in turn from the bottle as they jolted along, and Rupe didn't know whether the whiskey made him feel better or worse. He was thinking about breaking the news to Dad. On top of Mom's death, this would be almost too much for Frank to bear.

It was more than Rupe himself wanted to endure, for that matter. Nothing would ever be the same with Jord gone. They had shared everything, all the way up to maturity, from the New England hills to the plains of Kansas. His mind was back in that long broad valley of Otter Creek, the Green Mountains massed majestically on the eastern skyline, the Taconics humped on the west. Rupe could see the woodlands they had roved, the stone-bedded streams they had fished, the shaded pools and sparkling clean lakes they had swum in. He tasted maple sap and sugar in early spring, saw the long green meadows of summer stretching between dark-wooded slopes, and smelled the burning leaves in autumn when the maples flamed scarlet and gold on every hillside. But this was the Osawatomie. John Brown was gone but his war went on.

"He was right, Nick, John Brown was right," Rupert murmured. "You can't be neutral in Kansas."

"Of course you can't, Rupe," said Santell. "They say Old Brown's crazy and maybe he is, but he's right about a helluva lot of things."

They rode on, rocking and swaying in the dust-laden heat, and Rupert glanced back from time to time to see that Jordan was riding all right back there.

A stumpy, gray-whiskered man named Plosser hailed them from a roadside shanty: "Carrick's slavers went a hellity-hoopin' past here awhile back, snortin' fire and brimstone, howlin' like mescal-drunk Injuns."

Rupe Maitland swore softly. "Whip 'em up, Nick. We've got to travel."

"By God," breathed Nick Santell, "you don't suppose them stinkin' buzzards—"

"They're apt to do anythin', I guess," Rupe said, his teeth on edge. "We should've listened to Old John Brown. To Henry Holdcroft and Reef Bassett. To you, yourself, Nick."

"You goin' to join up, Rupe?"

"I want Early Hessler myself," Rupe said. "After that, I guess I'll join. There'll be no decent livin' here until the slavers are put down."

"Now you're talkin', Rupe," said Nick. "We'll chouse 'em right down across the Arkansas into Indian Territory."

Rupe Maitland was remembering the last time John Brown and his sons had called, over two years now. His mother and Melora crouched inside the house. Dad, Jord and himself out front as before, all scared except Dad, thinking they might die from this second visit. The big old man with the bushy beard and the burning, half-mad eyes, Bible in pocket, saber in hand.

"Quantrill and his slavers burned Lawrence down," John Brown said. "They murdered and raped, pillaged and looted, slaughtered and destroyed there. Are you goin' to set back and wait until they come to shoot your sons and rape your women and burn your homestead?"

"We'll fight when the time comes," Frank Maitland said calmly. "There's been evil on both sides. You and your men dragged five Doyles out of bed and cut them down with sabers in front of their womenfolk."

Rupert had expected that to bring wrath and destruction down on their heads, but the old man was strangely mild and controlled. "That was God's work," said John Brown. "God is a God of Wrath. . . ."

Rupe wondered where the old prophet was now, and all those hulking boys of his. Frederick, the yellow-haired giant, was reported dead, and Jason in prison. John, the first son, out of his mind, men said. Where were Owen, with the withered left arm; Oliver, the youngest and finest looking; Salmon and Watson? Then Rupe thought of his father alone at home, with Chance Carrick's crew on a drunken rampage in that direction, and a great fear gripped him through all the horror and grief of Jordan's death.

"Give 'em the whip, Nick," he said. "We've got to make time, with that bunch of bastards ahead of us."

Nick Santell nodded his head and plied the whiplash with cracking reports, the wagon leaping and lurching as the buckskins leaned into the traces. "It's the good people, the folks in the middle, who get hurt the most. You've got to take one side or the other, Rupe."

"I know that—now," Rupe Maitland said humbly. "It's good to have that much settled for you, Nick. But a hell of a price to pay."

Chapter 5

The sun was well past its zenith, Frank Maitland observed; the afternoon was getting along and he hadn't eaten since breakfast. After his visit to the grave, Frank had spent some time hoeing and weeding the garden, enjoying the smell of raw earth and the easy play of muscles, sun-warm limber and oiled with sweat. It was odd how a place could be so frying hot in summer and so deadly cold in winter, but that was Kansas for you. Now Frank was repairing tools and gear in the lean-to shed beside the barn, chewing tobacco as he worked with leisurely care and precision. He supposed he should eat something, but he wasn't hungry, and the thought of a lonely meal in the empty house depressed him.

Frank Maitland had been proud of his combination farm and ranch until Millicent died. After that it didn't seem to matter much; it was just a way of living. He'd been a farmer back in Vermont, and he was still a farmer out here. The boys liked riding and working cattle better, but he'd stick to the soil. He wondered if Milly ever had regretted marrying him, when she might have had Reuben Loomis, who worked in the bank and dressed nice and was probably president of the bank by now. Her family had preferred Reuben and thought Milly was foolish to marry a poor young farmer with fantastic ideas about pioneering out West. But Millicent had a mind of her own, and the strong, good-looking farmer stirred her as the pallid, starch-shirted bank clerk never could. She wanted to see the country, too, and Frank doubted if she'd ever regretted her choice in spite of the frontier dangers and hardships.

Strange how a man's life slipped away from him. When you're young, time means nothing; you think it will go on forever. With unlimited strength, energy and hope, you're sure you'll never grow old and die. Then marriage, children, hard, grinding work, and you're suddenly thirty. Life is a treadmill, the seasons pass ever faster, the years blend into one another. Forty comes before you know it, then middle age, and you feel that life and time have somehow cheated you. It hasn't turned out the way you dreamed and planned it in youth. The future and triumphs and better times have retreated before you, elusive fleeting shadows that you never quite catch up to, and now they are fading and vanishing forever. Life has gone too fast for you to grasp and hold and savor it. Your wife is dead, your children grow up, and you are all at once old—old and tired and alone.

Well, there was no sense railing against it. With Millicent he could have stood it all right, taken pleasure in the waning twilight years, but without her he felt empty as a spent shell, hollow and futile and desolate. You live twenty-eight years with a woman and she becomes part of you, and when she dies half of you dies with her, leaving only half a man to face the gray years. Frank Maitland was thankful for Rupe, Jord and Melora, proud and happy with them, but even three fine children could not compensate for the loss of his mate.

Frank turned his thoughts to the bitter growing strife in the Osawatomie country. Both sides had imported professional killers, the slavers first, the Free Staters following suit in desperation. Chance Carrick and Asa Sporn were gunfighters from Texas. Shaw Tattam, Huber Northrup and Elwood Kivett were adventurers and gunmen from the South Atlantic states. And there were others, all on the payroll of Clay Hessler. On the other side, Bassett and Holdcroft had a few professionals in their ranks. One spark was going to ignite all the powder before long, and set off a blast that would rock Kansas to its borders. One incident would change it from a succession of snipings, ambushings and street brawls to an open shooting war.

More and more of late, Frank Maitland was becoming convinced that a man's duty was to choose his side in this struggle and help fight it out. A Northerner from the New England stronghold of Abolitionists, the people he liked best were Free Staters, and he did not approve the principles of slavery. He had told John Brown it wasn't his cause, but Frank realized now it had to be his cause, if he were to live in this Territory. And the slavers, in this area at least, represented the wrong and evil, and did not truly represent the South.

The slavers had started the sniping from ambush, the cold-blooded murdering, and in many cases they warred against women and children as well as men. If folks were to live normally and safely in Kansas, the Southerners must be put down, beaten, whipped out of the country. From Frank Maitland's standpoint, the slavery issue was only incidental, almost irrelevant. It was fundamentally a battle between Good and Evil, Right and Wrong.

When Frank finally walked toward the long rambling log house, cleanly and substantially built, he noticed a dust cloud rising in the west toward Trayborough, such as a company of horsemen might make. Riders in that number today meant trouble for somebody, and he wondered if they were Carrick's slavers or Bassett's Free Staters. He thought, *We'll have to join up with Bassett and Holdcroft. I'll talk it over with the boys when they get home tonight. As Old Brown said, a man can't stay on the fence in Kansas.*

In the house, Frank Maitland buckled on his belt with the .44 Colt, spilled some extra shells into his pockets, and took the Henry rifle off its rack. It was a new repeater the boys had given him for his last birthday, a beautiful and powerful weapon in a country where single-shot Sharps, Spencers and Springfields were commonly used, and repeaters were almost unobtainable at this date. The Henry was a .44, taking the same shells as his handgun, which was another marked advantage. Frank felt better with the gun belt dragging at his hips and the Henry under his arm, but his heart sank coldly when he stepped outside and saw now, beyond any doubt, that the dust streamers were unfurling in his direction.

He surveyed the log house and the plank barn, making his decision quickly and heading for the latter. Frank Maitland didn't want the house shot up. It was the finest farmhouse around, and Millicent had taken pride and comfort in it. Real glass in all the windows, and the pretty muslin curtains Milly had made. The house would be safer, harder to set fire to, but Frank didn't want it all scarred and riddled with bullets. From the barn he could cover the house and the entire front yard. He wished Rupe and Jord were with him; the three of them could stand off quite a force. But he'd do all right by himself with this new-style repeating rifle. That would slow them down and shake them back. They'd wonder where he got all that firepower.

Frank pulled the barn door shut and barred it, taking his stand at a narrow glassless slit of a window in the left front corner. It was a long, tedious wait, and he sweated freely in the close sultry confinement, biting off a fresh chew of tobacco to ease the parched dryness of his mouth and throat. Behind him the two milch cows stomped and munched restlessly in their stalls. Frank was glad the saddle horses were out in the pasture, with only old Noggin left in the corral.

The yellow dust cloud rolled closer; individual riders began to emerge from it, and Frank recognized the towering Chance Carrick with his vulture face in the lead. Slowing and spreading out as they approached the farmstead, others came into view. Preacher Pratt, dressed all in black, gaunt and cadaverous with fanatical glowing eyes. Elwood Kivett, dapper and debonair as usual. Big Shaw Tattam, dark and ugly, massive and sullen in the saddle. Wide, husky Huber Northrup, immaculate and dignified as a gentleman on a social call. Whiplike Asa Sporn, the badman from Texas, reckless, wild and vicious in his range garb. A bearded man named Breen.

And others, yes. There was young Early Hessler, handsome and arrogant on a fine thoroughbred chestnut with white stockings. Karen's brother and a friend of Jordan and Rupert. Surely he wouldn't be here if they meant any harm. Once it had looked as if Rupe was going to marry Karen Hessler, and now Jord was keeping company with her. It didn't seem as if Early would take part in an attack on the Maitland place.

Sometimes Frank wondered why his sons hadn't married. At Rupe's age, Frank had been married for five years. Of course, there weren't too many nice girls to pick from on the frontier. He knew about Rupe's association with Dodie Deneen, although nothing ever was said about it. Too bad in a way that Rupe couldn't marry her, for women like Dodie sometimes made fine wives.

There were about twenty riders all told and their wary, fanned-out advance indicated no friendly visit, no favorable intentions. "Halloo-oo, the house!" they were calling. He caught the mockery in their ringing tones, wondering how many innocent farmers had answered that call, to be shot to pieces in front of wives and children on their own doorsteps? Anger stirred and mounted red and hot in Frank Maitland, throbbing in his temples. *Come on, you cowardly young curs!* he thought. *Your kind's brave only in wolf packs. If you want trouble, I'll give you all I can, and it'll be a bellyful for some of you.*

A rider in a red shirt threw up his rifle and fired at the house, smashing a front window. He was reloading when Frank lined the Henry and shot him out of the saddle, the horse bolting and Red Shirt lying where he had fallen. The others, whirled and scattered, shooting at the barn, their lead tearing and chewing at the wooden door and plank walls. Frank hammered back at them, aiming, squeezing off and levering, the carbine spanging with clean power and slamming back hard against his solid right shoulder. A pinto pony went down, rolling in a shower of reddish dirt, and the rider scrambled crablike for shelter. Some had dismounted behind the great live oaks before the house, while others dropped behind the stone fence, circled the corral, or drifted into the cottonwoods and willows along the creek.

With the repeater, Frank could hold them off in front, but he couldn't prevent them from swinging around back and setting fire to the barn, burning him out into the open.

Their wild howling sounded drunken, however, and maybe they wouldn't think of that.

"Come on, you drunken rabble," Frank said softly through his teeth. "Come on, scum and riffraff! You don't like it so well when somebody's shootin' back at you, I guess. You aren't so brave when you're gettin' shot at, are you?"

They were firing from cover, bullets beating at the barn, splintering through the door, raking the walls, but Frank was fairly secure behind the heavy corner beams, his slitted window deep silled enough to afford protection. Their marksmanship wasn't formidable; some time passed before they put a slug into that narrow open window.

Frank Maitland calmly chewed his tobacco and held his fire, waiting for a target, throwing occasional shots to keep the raiders pinned down. His predicament was grave but not hopeless. More than anything else he feared fire. Perhaps someone would hear the shooting and summon Reef Bassett's band to the rescue. Maybe Rupe and Jord would get some warning in town and come home at once.

A horse screamed outside in the corral, and wrath boiled up in Frank Maitland. They had shot old Noggin, the plough horse.

Frank strode to the rear of the barn, the cows lowing plaintively as he passed. Peeping from a small square window at the back, he saw a string of riders file into sight. Frank took careful aim and triggered smoothly, the Henry kicking back, the muzzle-flash flickering palely in the sunshine. The front man was spilled from his saddle and dragged along the ground, the mount breaking into a runaway gallop as his foot caught in the stirrup. The others wheeled into instant flight, with Frank firing after them. Reloading the rifle, he ran back to his front corner loophole.

They were driving in from the foreground, a few mounted, the rest on foot. It occurred to Frank that they knew he was alone, having seen Rupe and Jord in Trayborough. Firing fast, he checked the rush, dropping a horse and winging the man as he ran away, driving the others back. But he couldn't go on covering both the front and the rear. Better stick to this corner and keep them away from the front door. They couldn't get in from the back. All they could do was start a fire there, and that would finish him.

It wasn't long before they did this. They probably carried coal oil for the purpose. Flames soared up the rear wall, crackling and eating hungrily at the dry timber. The barn filled chokingly with smoke, and the cows began to bawl piteously. Heat waves beating at him, Frank led the frightened animals from their stalls to the forward end of the building. The fire had burned its way inside now, the scarlet and amber flames leaping and spreading rapidly, the smoke becoming dense and suffocating. Soon the fire would be feeding on the dried hay in the loft, and Frank would have to break outside in under the enemy gun muzzles. Already his eyes were smarting and watering, spasms of coughing racked him, and the scorching heat increased with a remorseless roaring intensity.

The two cows were bellowing, thrashing about, butting their heads into the wall, crazed with terror. Frank opened the door enough to let them burst outside, and heard the guns racketing as the slavers shot down the cattle in the yard. The searing heat and gagging smoke were too much to endure any longer. The flames had reached the hayloft, and the interior was one vast bonfire. He'd have to go out and get shot down like those cow-critters, but he'd damn sure take a few more of the vandals with him.

Frank thought of how hard he and the boys had labored to build this barn, and the rage in him blazed as hot as the surrounding fire. Weeping, choking and retching, he stumbled to the door, the Henry rifle fully loaded and ready. He had to break out before the smoke got him. The rear end of the roof was caving in, cascading fiery sparks and flaring fragments.

Frank Maitland slipped outside into the brilliant sunlight, gulping in fresh open air, stumbling over one of the dead animals as shots streaked in at him from all sides, the lead whining close, tugging at his clothing. From his knees, Frank fired the Henry as fast as he could pull the trigger and work the lever, unhit by that first volley only because he had tripped and fallen flat. Coming up into a

wide-spread crouch, Frank went on blasting with the
carbine, ringed in by a full hundred-and-eighty-degree arc
of enemy gunfire.

Finally the snarling bullets found and smashed him,
with lightning strokes in the head and body and leg, driving
him over backward into a loose roll against the carcass of
the second cow. Floundering there, still gripping the
Henry, sweaty, grimed face turning against the dead cow's
flank, Frank Maitland felt the life and light wrenched out of
him, and knew nothing more as crushing blackness closed
in.

Chapter 6

Three riders had joined the wagon when rifle fire crackled out ahead of them, rolling and echoing like summer thunder in the east. Nick Santell lashed the buckskins into a run, and Rupe Maitland leaned forward on the bucking seat, praying silently and swearing aloud into the rushing dusty breeze. The horsemen galloped alongside of the careening wagon: Old Sam Sybert, a burly gray-mustached man gone to fat, and his chubby round-faced son Lemuel; and one-eyed Poke Vetter, lean and leathery in his greasy buckskins, a veteran mountain man and Indian fighter. They were Free State neighbors and friends of the Maitland family.

The gunfire went on, rising and falling faintly through the thunder of hoofs and clatter of wheels, and then smoke billowed up blackly into the brassy blue sky, mushrooming evilly in the sunshine. Rupe moaned like a man in mortal agony, and Nick made the lash sing and crack over the straining, lathered team. The riders pressed on ahead, firing their handguns as they neared the Maitland place. Rupe and Nick emptied their revolvers into the air, to convey the illusion of a large force coming, and Rupe reloaded both weapons while Nick urged the horses on with voice and whip. The three horsemen halted to reload and the wagon overtook them, the party sweeping onward in a body and now saving their shells.

It was all over when they swung into view of the farmstead, the barn a towering mass of flames and smoke, the raiders disappearing into the timber to the north. Rupe groaned, grinding his teeth in helpless fury. As the wagon hurtled on into the trampled farmyard, past two dead horses and the red-shirted corpse of a man, Rupe jumped down before the wagon stopped, racing toward the blast-furnace heat of the burning barn. His father was a blood-soaked bundle beside the dead cows, empty brass from the Henry littered around him. Seared and breathless, Rupert lifted Frank's body and carried him away from the blaze toward the house, thinking, *O God, this is too much! Jord and Dad both, in one afternoon. No, God, please God, let him be alive.*

By some miracle, Frank Maitland was still alive, Rupe discovered after laying him down on the leather couch in the parlor. Poke Vetter made a hasty examination and declared that Frank would live and recover completely. "Don't seem possible nohow, with all them shootin' at him, but Frank ain't hit bad at all. None a them wounds is real bad, Rupe. I reckon his time just hadn't come yet."

Proficient from long experience with gunshot wounds, Poke Vetter called for water and clean cloths and whiskey, and went to work at once. One bullet had furrowed Frank's scalp, enough to knock him out but not to damage the skull, Poke reported. Another had passed through his side between the short ribs and the hip-bone, touching neither, clean as a whistle. The third slug had ripped through his left thigh without breaking the bone. Frank remained unconscious while Poke Vetter deftly bathed and sterilized the wounds, dressed and bound them, neat and secure.

"Never saw nothin' like it," Poke said, mild wonder in his one good eye. "Hit three times and not a bone broke, not a chunka lead left in him. The Lord musta figured on sparin' Frank today after already takin' Jord."

With Frank comfortably at rest, they had a drink and went outside to survey the battleground and watch the barn burn down, the shed going with it. There was another dead slaver out in back, Lem Sybert told them after his circuit of the place, and from the signs, Frank had killed or wounded some others, too.

"Ol' Frank put up one helluva fight," observed Sam Sybert.

"He's one hell of a man, Sam," said Nick Santell quietly.

"This'll fetch Reef Bassett and his boys," Poke Vetter said. "I'd like to git on the trail, soon as we have men enough to run 'em down right."

They unloaded the wagon and laid Jord away in the cool depths of the root cellar for the present. "We won't tell Dad right off," Rupe said. "He's had enough for one day."

"He'll probably know, anyway," Nick muttered. "He'll read it in our faces most likely."

"Well, we can't help that, Nick."

The Syberts unslung their ropes to drag the dead horses away for future burial, and brought in the corpse from behind the barn. A former Missouri outlaw named Glisson placed the dead man with the red-shirted one under a tarpaulin. Poke Vetter rode out to bring in the Maitland saddle horses, and Nick Santell set about cooking a meal. Rupert, fit for nothing but killing in his present state, sat on the porch cradling a whiskey bottle and staring sightlessly across the plains. When the fire burned itself out and cooled off some, there'd be two cows to butcher and dress.

Sandy, the big collie, came in from running the fields and muzzled Rupe's knees, and Rupe stroked his golden head, saying, "They even killed old Nog, Sandy. It's a good thing you weren't around to get shot up, boy."

An hour later Frank Maitland recovered consciousness and talked with Rupe and Nick. "You boys must have got here just about in time," he said, with a gaunt wisp of a smile.

"No, they were runnin' when we pulled in, Dad. They figured you were finished."

"So did I. What brought you back so early, Rupe?"

Rupert shrugged. "Nothin' in town. You recognize any of them, Dad?"

Frank inclined his bandaged head and named the ones he had seen. Then he asked the question they'd been dreading: "Where's Jord?"

"He stayed in town," Rupe said, looking at the floor,

while Nick became suddenly interested in his stubby freckled hands.

"Karen, I suppose," Frank murmured. "Who patched me up so good?"

"Poke Vetter. The Syberts are here too, Dad."

"Good neighbors." Frank looked at his son-in-law. "Melora with you, Nick?"

"No, she's comin' out later, I think."

Frank blinked gravely at them. "You boys are actin' kind of odd, or else it's the hole in my head. Somethin' you want to tell me, Rupe?"

"Why no, Dad. Do you want a drink?"

Frank nodded and Nick hastened after the whiskey. Frank stared up with somber steadiness at his big lanky son. "Rupe, you sure Jord stayed in town?"

"Sure, Dad. You know how he—"

"No, Rupe. I can tell different. Somethin' happened in there today. What was it, Rupe? I've got to know. It's Jord, isn't it? Jord's hurt—or dead?"

Rupert bowed his tawny head, eyes scalded and throat choking-full. No use in lying any more. Nothing to do but tell the truth, for the knowledge was already agonizing his father's brown eyes. "Dead, Dad." Rupe forced the words out, and went on to tell about it, in a strained broken voice unrecognizable as his own.

Frank Maitland took it as well and stolidly as a man could, the grief deep in his eyes and cutting cruel lines in his gaunted face. "Well, Rupe," he said, after an anguished silence, "I guess we know which side we're on now, don't we?" He accepted the glass of whiskey from Nick Santell. "Thanks, Nick. Maybe you boys better leave me alone, for a little."

"Dad, you're goin' to be all right?" Rupe said, with desperate urgency. "You—you—"

"Sure I'll be all right, Rupe," said Frank. "You brought Jord home, didn't you? That's good. We'll bury him beside his mother. Now boys, I—"

They nodded jerkily and turned away from the couch, their eyes blinded and streaming, leaving Frank alone with his grief.

Toward evening the Lambert's big Murphy wagon rumbled into the farmyard, Mrs. Lambert handling the reins with Melora at her side, while True Lambert and young Joe Gayle rode their horses ahead of the vehicle. The wagon was crammed with household furnishings and goods, and True Lambert said, "The fightin's already begun in Trayborough. A dozen or more dead already, and most of 'em Free Staters. They say Atchinson's marchin' on the town with two hundred slavers, so we decided to pull out. Most all of our people are movin' out."

"Plenty of room here, True," said Rupe Maitland. "You're more than welcome and we're glad to have you. Dad got shot up some, but he's goin' to be all right. Your missus can keep house, True, and Melora can take care of Dad."

"Much obliged, Rupe. We'll be buildin' as soon as we can." True Lambert blinked and swallowed hard, stroking his horse's mane. "That was pure hell about Jord. There ain't much a man can say, Rupe. And I'm sorry to see your barn burned out, but we'll put up another one." He was a stocky, gnarled stump of a man, blunt and steadfast.

Melora had dropped from the wagon box into her husband Nick's wiry arms, and now she turned to her brother with anxious, stricken blue eyes. "Rupe, is Dad really all right?" She was a pretty blonde girl with her mother's eyes and the Maitland smile, a perky snub nose and a normally tanned rosy complexion. Her face was drawn and ashen now, marked deep with Jord's death and fear for her father. Melora was going to have a baby, and she wondered if it was fair to bring a child into this war-torn world.

"Dad's goin' to be fine, Mel," Rupe assured his sister, holding her hard and briefly. "Go on in and see him. He'll sure be glad you're here." Melora nodded, smiled bravely and ran into the log house.

"We brought all your stuff along with ours, Nick," True Lambert was saying. "The slavers are takin' Trayborough over, and that's for sure. There's no more livin' for us Northerners in that town. It'd be plain suicide to stay there."

Joe Gayle, a large, amiable young man in his early twenties, laid a friendly brawny arm on Rupe's rangy shoulders. "We're goin' after 'em, ain't we, Rupe? They say Reef Bassett's on his way out here. I—I reckon you know how I felt about Jord. He was the best boy I ever knew, Rupe."

Rupert nodded. "Thanks for helpin' the folks pack and move out, Joe. We'd better get the wagon unloaded while it's daylight."

They went to work unloading at once, and Hester Lambert followed Melora inside the house. The barn was a smoldering, reeking mound of charred rubble now. The Syberts had the dead cows strung up on the corral rails and were dressing them out, with the expert assistance of Poke Vetter, who was back with the saddle horses.

At dusk they heard the hoofbeats of an oncoming column, and everyone withdrew to the interior of the house, blowing out lamps and taking their stands at the windows, rifles in hand and six-guns belted on.

Then the call "Free Staters and friends!" came from the outer shadows and the company rode directly into the yard.

"It's Bassett and Holdcroft," announced Joe Gayle from his corner window. "With about twenty men, it looks like." Rupert led them outside to greet and exchange stories with their allies.

Reef Bassett, his red-rock face harsh and stern, his iron jaws jutting, listened to Rupe's story and went into his own: "Atchinson's taken Trayborough. We'll be movin' against the town in a few days. I've got men out scourin' the country for recruits. Right now we're after that crew of Chance Carrick's that hit you folks here. With luck we can cut 'em off before they double back to Trayborough. I reckon some of you men'll want to ride along."

They all wanted to, but Rupe pointed out the necessity of leaving someone behind to protect the farm, the womenfolk, and the wounded Frank Maitland. This was obvious; yet no one wished to stay at home. Rupe and Nick Santell insisted on their right to go, since Carrick's outfit had struck their family. Henry Holdcroft wanted Poke

Vetter for his tracking skill and knowledge of the country-side. Reef Bassett selected Joe Gayle because of his youth and strength. It was finally agreed that True Lambert and the Syberts should remain on the spread, much to their profound disgust.

Henry Holdcroft, thin, keen and sharp-faced, clapped Lambert and Sam Sybert on the back and smiled reassuringly at young Lem Sybert. "You'll get all the fightin' you want, boys, before this week is up," he promised. "It'll take a full-scale battle to rout them out of Trayborough. We'll all get our bellies full of it in the next few days."

Melora and Mrs. Lambert were stuffing saddlebags with food and extra shells, and Rupert took Dad's Henry repeater and Jord's .44 Remington along with his own Colt. Quick mask-faced farewells were made, and the riders mounted up and took off toward the northern timber where the raiders had vanished that afternoon. The dusk was thickening, but the moon tonight would be nearly at the full.

The war was on in real earnest now, Rupe Maitland thought, astride his bay gelding, with Nick riding the star-faced black. It wouldn't cease until one side or the other was driven from the burning plains and wild woodlands of Kansas. Rupe thought, *Old John Brown and his sons should be here. Old John would be right in his glory, with a war like this building up in the Osawatomie.*

Chapter 7

The trail of so many horsemen—the cocksure Carrick having made no effort to obscure it—was easy enough to follow, even at night. They moved on into the broken wilderness of the northern Osawatomie, with the clop of hoofs, jingle of bridle chains, creak of leather, and the clank of canteens. The moon had risen to light the earth, and the Free Staters traveled at a brisk, steady pace with patch-eyed Poke Vetter at the point of the column, the course as clearly defined to him as a highway through the sparse-wooded forest. The smell of horses, sweated saddles and flannel, oiled steel, tobacco and saddle soap rode with them into the cool fresh greenery of trees, brush and ferns.

"They could be headin' for Hessler's Pond, Nick," said Rupe Maitland thoughtfully.

Nick Santell nodded. "If they don't swing back toward Trayborough, that's a pretty good bet, Rupe. You know where it is, don't you?"

"I've been up there with Karen. They've got a huntin' camp at the headwaters of the Cygne."

"It must be hell in town. Eastlach tells me they killed Brownlee and his wife with their kids lookin' on." Nick spat viciously. "They got a lot to answer for, Rupe."

Eastlach, his thin young face solemn, reined in beside Rupe. "They say Atchinson's men took over the saloons and got so roarin' drunk they was even shootin' people on their own side. They stared shovin' around and tearin' the clothes off the girls in the Redwing. I heard that Dodie

43

Deneen shot one of 'em, and they whipped her half to death in front of the whole mob."

Rupe Maitland winced as if under a lash himself. He scarcely had thought of Dodie since leaving her so abruptly, and this news did not move him as it ordinarily would have. Since Jordan's death, nothing seemed to touch him or to matter like it used to. His sensitivity was blunted, his sympathetic nature turned hard and cold and uncaring. The vision of Dodie being whipped in public was a disagreeable and distasteful one, but it failed to rouse Rupe as it would have once. Instead of firing him with hate and fury, it left him faintly ill, otherwise almost indifferent. As if the shameful thing had happened to a stranger, an unknown woman.

Dodie never would give in to them, Rupe thought. She'd get herself killed, as sure as anything. Or kill herself, if they took her by force. Dodie Deneen was a woman of high, fierce pride and independence.

"Atchinson's Assassins," snarled Nick Santell, "the scum of Missouri and the Indian Territory. Bushwhackers from the Platte, and cutthroat Kickapoo renegades. The filth of the whole frontier."

They pushed on, a forced march all the way under the branch-latticed moonlight, with intervals of walking and trotting, leading, and rests for watering. The sharp fragrance of spruce and jackpine mingled with the milder odors of cedar and oak, juniper, beech and hickory, and along the creeks and rivulets, willow and cottonwood. Brush tearing at horses and riders in places, and boulders looming gray and jagged through the moonlit thickets. A grim march of vengeance in the balmy night.

It was between eleven and midnight, Rupe estimated from an upward glance at the Big Dipper, when Poke Vetter and Reef Bassett raised their arms to halt the cavalcade in a grassy basin. The Southerners had split up here, the larger party branching off into the southwest as if to circle back to Trayborough, a smaller group swinging north and west in the general direction of the upper Cygne River. This northwest trace upheld Rupe's hunch, and he felt fairly certain that Early Hessler was conducting a detachment to the hunting lodge on Hessler's Pond, as they liked to call it.

"Only five or six went that way," Reef Bassett said, studying the signs. "We'll let 'em go and try to head off the main bunch. They'll all wind up in Trayborough sooner or later, anyway."

"I'd like to follow this trail, Reef," said Rupe Maitland, pointing in a northwesterly direction. "I think it's Early Hessler and his friends."

"You can't go alone, Rupe," protested Henry Holdcroft.

"I'm with Rupe," put in Nick Santell quickly. Poke Vetter and Joe Gayle volunteered likewise, and young Eastlach said he'd like to string along with them.

Bassett and Holdcroft conferred briefly, and Reef said gruffly, "All right, Rupe, you five boys go along north and good luck to you. Just be sure and get back in time for the attack on Trayborough, because we're goin' to need every man and every gun we can round up."

"We'll be there, Reef," promised Rupert, and the posse separated without further words or loss of time. Rupe figured that along with Early Hessler would be Sporn and Tattam, Kivett and Northrup and possibly Chance Carrick. The leaders, the worst of the lot, and Rupe wanted to get at them so badly he felt that his hunch must be correct.

After two hours on the new track, Rupe was surer than ever they were lining out for the Cygne headwaters and the Hessler cabin. They pressed on through the tilted woodlands and scrubby clearings. Several times on stony surfaces they might have lost the trail if old Poke Vetter's one eye hadn't been supernaturally sharp, quick and sure. Old-timers always said Poke could trail a squirrel across naked flint rock, and Rupe was inclined to believe them after this uncanny exhibition. "Hellfire, I'm more'n half-Injun, son," Poke Vetter said. "Hunted and trapped up north with Sioux and Blackfeet and married more squaws than most men ever have white females. Injun women are a whole lot easier to git along with than white women."

At last they were climbing through scattered pine and fir toward the crooked ridges and rocky hills that marked the headwater region. Hours after midnight they came out upon a height of land overlooking Hessler's Pond, the flat moon-silvered sheen of it glimmering through the trees and brush. It occupied a shallow basin, ringed in by forested ridges and hillocks, a picturesque spot that reminded Rupert of his trips here with Karen Hessler in younger, more romantic days. Tethering their mounts in a pine grove well back on the rise, the five men prowled forward on foot with their rifles, alert against the possibility of outguards. Encountering none, it became evident that the slavers scornfully ignored the threat of pursuit, feeling secure in their own superiority.

The snug log cabin stood on a small open plateau above the lakeshore, and the flooding moonlight showed six unsaddled horses in the pole corral at the left, with a long woodshed on the right side. The cabin, unlighted and silent, faced the pond, but there were windows and a door in the back. A seldom-used pleasure camp, it was constructed and furnished better than most of the permanent homes in the region.

Hunkering down behind brush-shrouded boulders a hundred yards above and behind the log house, Rupe and the others tried to formulate a satisfactory plan of campaign. As much as Rupe wanted to kill those men, the idea of slaughtering them in their sleep was utterly repugnant to him, and his companions felt the same way about it for the most part.

"The damn fools didn't even post a sentry," Rupe grumbled.

"Probably not," Poke Vetter said, munching his tobacco. "But we can't just take that for granted, Rupe. They *might* have a guard down there. Now if we was Injun-smart, we'd snake down and butcher 'em in bed, but bein' more or less civilized, we got to give 'em a fightin' chance, I reckon. Which nobody ever deserved less than them ornery varmints."

Poke spat judiciously and went on: "Now why don't I slip down there and turn loose them horses, while you boys kinda surround the place? If nobody jumps me and the horses don't wake 'em up, we'll bust a few windows and give 'em a chance to pull on their boots and grab their guns and shoot back at us. Then we'll feel better about the whole goddamn thing, and the rest of it'll take care of itself."

"I hate to be too fair with that bunch," Nick Santell said. "They're murderers, and they don't deserve anythin' better than murder themselves."

"That's what I say," declared Eastlach. "It don't make sense to risk our own lives just to give them slavers an even break."

Joe Gayle grinned good-naturedly. "I know just how you boys feel, but how would we feel after we'd shot them sleepin' in bed? That ain't apt to leave a good taste in a decent man's mouth."

"Well, Rupe, it's your party and it ought to be your say," Nick Santell said, his honed-down features sharp and bitter in the moonbeams. "You got more at stake than we have in this deal."

Rupe Maitland was thoughtful and troubled, stroking the smooth stock of the Henry rifle. "I can see both sides, boys," he said, slow and soft. "And I could argue both sides, but I guess I'll have to go along with Poke and Joe. I want to kill Early Hessler more'n I ever thought I'd want to kill anybody, but I sure don't want to kill him in bed."

"I see what you mean, Rupe, and most likely you're right," Nick muttered. "We'll wake the slavin' skunks up and give 'em their chance."

"Sure, boys," drawled Poke Vetter, touching the black patch over his eyeless socket. "They oughta know why they're dyin' and who's killin' 'em. A lot more satisfyin' that way."

With Poke creeping down to the corral, Eastlach was to stay behind to cover him and the rear, while Joe Gayle took the left wing beyond the corral and Nick Santell the right flank from the woodshed. Rupe Maitland would swing around on the lakeside to command the front of the cabin. Their strategy settled on, they started moving their various ways, treading slow and light, utilizing all the available shelter of brush, trees and rocks. The moonlight that had been such a boon on the trail was a curse to them now.

In the stillness, Rupe Maitland could hear the minute night life of the earth he was crawling along—the thin hum of insects on the air, the mournful croaking of frogs in the marshes below. Fireflies traced erratic greenish white patterns about him. An owl hooted from the ridge, and a loon called weirdly across the water. The horses stirred and chomped in the corral, pawing the ground and swishing their tails against the flies. Glancing back, Rupe saw Nick waving toward the shed. Before him birches shimmered palely along the shoreline.

Completing his arc, Rupe maneuvered into a rock-sheltered position that gave him a clear field of fire to the front of the camp. The night air smelled cleanly of balsam, birches and lake water, and Rupe remembered lazy sun-bright days and clear moonlit nights on that porch with Karen. Memories threaded with the sweet fire of desire, but fretted with endless frustration and unfulfillment. The dark vivacious girl flirting, smiling archly, teasing, yet always aloof. Angrily, Rupe put her out of mind, and levered a shell into the chamber of the Henry. The thought of Dodie Deneen recurred then, but he didn't want that either. Thinking of her would always bring back the horror of Jordan's death in the square at Trayborough. Unfair to Dodie, but Rupert couldn't help it. He waited for the rushing trample of hoofs that would come when Poke turned loose the horses.

Instead of that it was a gunshot from out beyond the corral, a flashing roar that split the stillness and blared almost into Joe Gayle's face, illuminating the brush and leaf patterns and the bearded face of Breen, the man Rupe had struck down in the crowded plaza. The Southerners hadn't been so stupid and careless after all, and Joe Gayle, who wanted to give them an even shake, was down with his head nearly blown off his rugged shoulders. The horses were frightened into a plunging, bucking panic.

Rupe saw the lightning of Poke Vetter's gun streak from the corral bars, as he lined and let go with the Henry, taking the recoil and levering swiftly and slamming another shot at Breen's fading muzzle light. Poke Vetter must have put his first slug home, for Breen was down thrashing in the undergrowth, grunting and groaning for a moment, then silent and motionless.

The cabin was almost instantly awake with flame torching from the windows, as Nick Santell opened up from the woodshed and Poke Vetter threw close-range shots from his handgun into the rear of the structure. Glass shattered thinly under the crash of gunfire, and lurid streaks laced the night. Rupe was hammering away with his repeater, pouring lead into the windows from which flashes were spurting. Bullets searched the slope, crackling through brush and snarling off rock surfaces, chipping at tree trunks, clipping off twigs and leaves. From the hillside behind the cottage came the spaced booming of Eastlach's .50 caliber Sharps.

This thing sure backfired on us, Rupe Maitland thought wryly. *Trying to be fair, we handed them every advantage. They could hold that log fort a long time, unless we get lucky and score more shots than we've any license to. They've got some repeating rifles in there and I've got the only one out here. We sure mucked this up, and young Joe Gayle has already paid for it.*

Rupert was reloading when big Shaw Tattam burst out the front door like a maddened monster and came charging down the path with guns blazing in either hand. Bullets screeched off the boulders, and one ricochet blinded Rupe with a stinging slash of stone dust, driving him backward as a red-hot iron seared the right side of his skull. Blind and half-stunned, Rupe reeled in the brush, and Shaw Tattam came bounding on with both six-guns flaring. Dropping the empty rifle, Rupe clawed at his holstered Colt, but Tattam had him cold and dead—until Tattam's hammers clicked on empty shells. With a panting curse, the giant hurdled the rocks and bulled in to club Rupe with his right-hand gun.

Rupe recovered enough to roll his head away from the wicked blow, the gun barrel smashing down on his left shoulder with paralyzing force, and Tattam's driving bulk knocking Rupe spinning and sprawling on his back. Shocked half-senseless, his left shoulder feeling crushed and broken, Rupe dragged his Colt from the sheath, but Shaw Tattam was on top of him, kicking the gun out of his hand, stomping at Rupe's chest and face. With a frenzied twist, Rupe rolled and locked his arms about those great stamping legs, clinging and heaving with all his explosive strength, upsetting the big man.

They rolled in a wild thrashing tangle, with Tattam chopping at Rupe with a gun barrel, but Rupe came out on top with an elbow in Tattam's throat, smashing the big black head back against a stone. Breaking away and scrambling clear, Rupe raked Jord's Remington out of his waistband, just as Tattam came lunging along the ground at him. Rupe whipped the barrel across Tattam's bulling head, beating him facedown in the dirt, but the slaver's momentum flung Rupe flat on his shoulder blades again, the air torn from his agonized lungs.

Shaw Tattam should have been unconscious from that clout on the skull, but he was not. Scrabbling about in the ferns, he came up with Rupe's Colt and swung around snarling, just as Rupert struggled to his knees and lifted the Remington. Both guns were coming to bear, but Rupe thumbed his hammer forward before Tattam could bring his weapon into line. The flame speared straight at Shaw Tattam's dark ugly face, rocking his head far back as the .44 bucked up in Rupe's hand. Tattam's late shot flickered skyward as the giant lurched violently, then sagged to earth, his shattered skull in the gravel, his blasted face upturned to the stars.

Sick and retching, Rupe Maitland stumbled to his feet, picking up and holstering the Colt that had kicked out of Tattam's dying hand, searching for the Henry. The firing around the cabin seemed to have slackened. Rupe found the rifle and was reaching down for it, when his aching head burst suddenly in a white-hot flash of light. He pitched forward into bottomless blackness. . . .

When Rupe came back to life, Nick Santell was crouching beside him and the night was strangely still. "What happened, Nick?" he asked, wondering at the silence.

"They got away, three of 'em did. Breen's dead with Joe Gayle and you got Tattam here and Piche's dead in the cabin. But the ones we wanted got away. Hessler and Kivett and Northrup, I think. Poke got hit, not too serious, but it knocked him out for a while. He's up on the hill with Eastlach. Can you walk all right, Rupe?"

"Yeah, I guess so. It's just my head and shoulder." Rupert got up, slow and careful, his head ringing and his left shoulder in a vise of pain. "Sure, I can make it, Nick."

They walked slowly around the cabin and up the long, gradual slope. The corral was empty now, the reek of powder smoke still hovering about the log house. Nick said bitterly. "We carried Joe up. There ain't much left of his face and head."

"I know, Nick. We played it wrong, and I'm to blame for it."

"Don't blame yourself, boy. If Joe's number was up, it was up, that's all."

They were halfway up to where Eastlach was waiting with the wounded Vetter, when a quick onrushing beat of hoofs drummed the upper slope. A single horseman was in a headlong charge at Eastlach's position, coming with hurricane speed. Eastlach rose to face this unexpected threat from the rear, firing his carbine and then Poke Vetter's, but horse and rider swept on untouched. There was no time to reload, and Eastlach went to his handgun, but the oncoming mount and man seemed impervious to lead. Rupe and Nick, unable to shoot for fear of hitting Eastlach and Vetter, fanned out on either side to try for angled shots. But there wasn't time; the horseman was almost on top of Eastlach.

Moonlight touched the gaunt maniacal face of the black-garbed rider, as an insane scream went up from him. It was Preacher Pratt, running straight on into Eastlach's gun muzzle, with a long saber uplifted for the stroke. Eastlach, his revolver emptied, scrambled aside to draw Pratt away from the prostrate Vetter. The saber slashed, a wicked shining arc in the moonbeams, shearing through Eastlach's skull and cutting him down in a dark gout of blood.

With a mad shriek of triumph, Preacher Pratt drove on downhill at the other two men, swinging his bloodied blade and veering toward Nick Santell as they both opened fire on him. Nick dropped his single-shot rifle and drew his revolving pistol, while Rupe went on shooting with the Henry repeater. The horse screamed, even higher than

Pratt, and went down in a threshing plunging fall, showering dust and flinging the Preacher clear and almost to Nick's feet. Throwing down with his .44 Colt, Nick Santell blasted away at that black-clad, writhing body until his gun was empty and Preacher Pratt, the most bloodthirsty of all Atchinson's Assassins, was shot to pieces against the smoking earth.

"That crazy saberin' murderer!" Nick panted, reloading as Rupe crossed the slope to join him. "Where the hell do you suppose he came from?"

"I don't know." Rupe looked down at the riddled fanatic with a shudder, his spine still tingling and his scalp tight and bristling, nausea stirring in his stomach. "I was beginnin' to think bullets wouldn't touch him or his horse, either."

They climbed on to where Poke Vetter was lying, with Joe Gayle's body wrapped in a blanket and young Eastlach dead in his blood. Eastlach had brought their horses down, while Nick went after Rupe. Now Nick got a blanket to roll Eastlach in, and they lashed the two dead boys across their saddles. Poke Vetter was conscious, chewing tobacco and watching them with his one eye, the bullet hole in his shoulder plugged and bandaged.

Feeling responsible for all of this, bowed under a burden of guilt and pain, Rupe Maitland squatted beside the old mountain man. "Can you ride, Poke?" he asked gently.

Poke Vetter nodded. "If I can't, Rupe, I ain't worth savin'."

They helped Poke onto his horse, swung into their own saddles, and started slowly homeward through the cheerless, early morning.

My hunch didn't work out so good, Rupe Maitland thought grimly. *Joe Gayle and Eastlach dead, and Poke wounded. We got four of them, Breen and Piche, Shaw Tattam and Preacher Pratt, but that's nowhere near enough to even up for Joe and Eastlach. And Early Hessler got off without a scratch.*

Chapter 8

They got back to the Maitland farm in the heat of afternoon, with their dead roped across the saddles and Poke Vetter drooping exhausted on his gray gelding, half-conscious and semidelirious from the long, grinding ordeal. Doc Kinderness was there to see Frank Maitland, and they turned Poke over to him, Melora and Mrs. Lambert preparing a bed for the wounded man. Untying the bodies of Eastlach and Joe Gayle, they laid them in the shade, after which they unsaddled the five horses and turned them into the corral.

True Lambert and the Syberts had not been idle in their absence. They had buried the dead horses and the two slavers as well, since it was unlikely that anyone would call to claim the corpses. True had made a coffin for Jord Maitland, while Sam and Lem Sybert cleaned up the blackened debris of the burned barn. The news from Trayborough had Atchinson's large force building barricades, digging breastworks, and preparing to defend the town they had taken. All Free Staters had been driven out or killed, and Doc Kinderness said he was spared simply because his professional services might be required. The slavers had hundreds of hired gunfighters, a veritable army, as well as a couple of cannons.

When Kinderness finished with Poke Vetter, he cleansed and sterilized the seared gash above Rupe's right ear and examined his left shoulder, which was badly bruised but not broken. The doctor said Frank was coming along well and Vetter would be all right. He didn't know

where the Eastlach and Gayle families had gone and
suggested that East and Joe be placed in temporary graves
here on the spread. More digging for Lambert and the
Syberts, who had prepared a grave for Jord on the knoll
next to his mother's, along with their other burial duties.

Rupert and Nick told Frank Maitland about their night
on the trail and the battle at Hessler's Pond, while the
women heated water for them to shave and bathe. Frank,
now undressed and bedded down in his own room, looked
aged, drawn and sunken, but declared that he was resting
easy and suffering little from his wounds. The death of Jord
had hit him harder than the enemy bullets. Parson
Theophilus Root was coming over to conduct a funeral
service for Jord. After shaving and bathing, Rupe and Nick
dressed for the ceremony in clean, dark clothes and went
out to greet the neighbors drifting in from farms and
ranches.

There were about thirty-five men and women on hand
when the minister arrived, and the yard was filled with
saddle horses, buggies and buckboards. Jordan lay in the
closed pine casket, its crudeness covered by black satin.
Theo Root was mercifully brief in his sermon. Rupe
scarcely heard a word of it, his ears attuned to the weeping
of women, his grief bitter and black within himself. Numb
with weariness, it all seemed unreal and dreamlike to him.
It was a relief to have the final Amen end it, and to help
carry the casket outside and up to the cedar-grown knoll
where the raw open grave waited. A relief to have the box
lowered on ropes into the ground, and the dirt from shovels
pelting down and covering it as the crowd slowly dispersed.

The smell of the soil lingered in Rupe's head and
caught in his throat, and for a long time he stood there,
towering starkly with the sun bright on his bare bent head,
staring at the freshly closed grave and at his mother's
tombstone nearby. When he turned away at last, he was
startled to see Karen Hessler standing in the shade of a
cedar tree, wearing a plain black riding habit, her dark
head bowed, her tear-wet face pale and haunted, etched
with misery and despair.

"What are you doin' here?" Rupe Maitland demanded, his voice as cold as his narrowed gray eyes.

"I had a right to come, Rupe," she said softly, humbly. "You know I did."

"Well, you'd better get back to Hessler Hall and to your own kind."

"They—they aren't my kind. Not any more, Rupe. I don't know what's come over Early. And my father, too."

"They haven't changed," Rupe told her. "They're just gettin' braver with Atchinson behind them."

"I—I don't uphold them in anything they're doing."

"You don't?" he mocked. "Why, I can't understand that, Karen. All they've done in the last twenty-four hours is murder Jord, attack my father about twenty-to-one, burn him out of the barn and put three bullets through him. Kill two more men and wound another at Hessler's Pond. Hardly a real day's work for your brother and those gallant gentlemen you were entertaining yesterday."

"Did you—kill Early?" asked Karen brokenly.

"Not yet," Rupe said grimly. "He got away, unfortunately. We did kill four of them, though. Shaw Tattam'll be missin' the next time you serve juleps."

"Rupe, I did something you may appreciate. I took Dodie Deneen away from that rabble of Atchinson's and brought her home with me."

"Generous and noble of you," Rupe drawled with satire. "The high-born lady and a dance-hall girl. Was she hurt much?"

"Badly enough, Rupe. She'll carry some of the scars, I'm afraid. But she's safe now; she's going to be all right."

"Until your brother and his friends get hold of her," Rupe said, lips thinning. "Then she'll wish Atchinson's dogs had killed her."

"They won't touch her, Rupe," promised Karen. "Nobody's going to harm her any more."

"You'd better get back home and see that they don't. They're probably back in Trayborough by now."

Karen made a small, hopeless gesture. "All right, Rupert. I won't bother you any more." Her deep dark eyes welled over, as she turned from him.

"Sorry, Karen," he said quickly. "I didn't mean to— Well, I do want to thank you for helpin' Dodie."

"You're in love with her, aren't you?" She wheeled and stared at him from wet, brilliant eyes.

"I—I don't know," Rupe mumbled, kicking at the turf. "I don't think so. From here on out I'm goin' to be too busy to love anybody, I guess."

"Rupe, what ever happened to us anyway? What came between us?" Her dark gaze was pleading, like her lips, offering more than ever before. One move from him and she'd have been in his arms.

Rupe looked at her with disgust. "What were you doin' with Jord? Playin' games?"

"No, Rupe, no!" Karen cried desperately. "I liked Jord, I was very fond of him. We—we had nice times together, but— But it was different, Rupe. It was never like it was with you."

"Get out!" Rupert said, his face bleak as bone. "Go on, go home. You're no good, Karen. You're worse than your brother, and he's rotten to the core!"

"You're wrong, Rupe—terribly wrong," she said, strangely quiet and calm now. "Sometime you'll know how wrong you are. I—I loved you, Rupe. I couldn't love Jord, too."

"Don't give me that, Karen," he protested dully. "You played the same way with both of us. A pretty, polite, lavender-and-lace affair. Don't call it love, Karen. Maybe it passes for that in the South, but it's no goddamn good in this country."

"That's not true, Rupert," murmured Karen again. "Some day you'll find out. But no matter, now. I shouldn't have come, but I *had* to. I'll leave now. I hoped you'd give me a chance, but I guess there's no use."

"Of course there isn't, even if you rated one," Rupe said. "I'm goin' to kill your brother, Karen. Maybe your father, too, before this is over. He's been financin' all these murders."

"Did it ever occur to you, Rupe, that you might die yourself?"

He smiled dimly. "Why sure, but what does it matter—now?"

"You mustn't feel that way, Rupert. I know how much you liked Jord, and how he worshiped you. But you still have a lot to live for, Rupe."

"We live or die the way it's written, so there's no sense worryin' about it."

"That fatalistic talk sounds too much like defeatism, Rupe."

He laughed softly. "Not in my case, Karen. I'll live long enough to do what I've got to do."

"Will you walk to the house with me, Rupe?" Looking up at him, she revealed the lovely line from her firm chin to the soft base of her throat, and in spite of himself Rupe hungered for the taste of those full red lips, the pressure of her lithe, softly rounded body against him, the warm closeness of her arms.

"No, Karen, I don't want to go down there—not yet," Rupe said kindly. "I don't feel like seein' anybody. I don't know how I've talked this long with you."

"I know, Rupe. I feel for you—and with you. So good-bye, for now."

"It's really good-bye this time, Karen," he said. "It's got to be."

From the shadow of the cedars, he watched her walk down the hillside with her lissome grace, and it wrenched something deep and hard inside him. Karen went into the house to pay her respects, emerging shortly to mount her thoroughbred bay mare and ride off into the westering sun toward Trayborough.

Rupe Maitland walked back along the hillock with that clawing, tearing grief locked within him, a sense of lonely desolation and the futility of life cold on his mind. At the far edge of the rise he stretched out full length in the grass, his face in the cool fresh greenness, his fingers raking deep into the sod, the pent-up tears flowing at last.

They were at supper in the Maitland farmhouse when two couriers from Reef Bassett's outfit rode in and announced that the Free State forces were gathering on

Mulehead Flats for the assault on Trayborough. Afterward, while True Lambert helped his wife with the dishes and Rupe Maitland talked to his father and Poke Vetter, the Santell couple sauntered down past the live oaks and the stone row to walk along the creek.

The sun was down, the afterglow still washing the western horizon in delicate fading pastel shades, with darkness growing swiftly on the broad plains. A mockingbird fluted with liquid sweetness from the cedar hummock behind the house, and somewhere a whippoorwill repeated its three clear insistent notes. Nick and Melora strolled westward until the soft pinks and lavenders dissolved on the skyline, and then turned back in under the thin-leafed cottonwoods and drooping willows, the creek swishing with silken music along its stony bed. Crickets chirped in the grass and frogs shrilled from outer marshlands. The mourning howl of a coyote rose in the distance, and Sandy barked sharply in response from the vicinity of the chicken house.

Melora and Nick hadn't seen much of one another since Friday. Things had happened too fast the last two days, a lifetime of action, strife and tragedy crowded into one weekend. They missed their own little home in Trayborough, even though by now it was probably reduced to ashes. They missed the privacy and routine pattern of their life together, with Nick driving a freight wagon and Melora keeping house. Her pregnancy didn't show yet, but she was more and more aware of it. And worried because it seemed a bad time and place to bear a child.

"Do you *have* to go, Nick?" asked Melora, her fingers tautening on the whipcord muscles of his arm.

"How can you ask that, Mellie? After what happened to Jord and your father?"

"I know, Nicky. But you went out last night and did your share, it seems to me. It doesn't seem fair to the baby—"

"It won't be any place for him to grow up in, Mel, if we don't run them slavers out. And we won't have any home to bring him up in."

Melora sighed wearily. "I suppose you're right, Nick. Maybe I'm too tired and upset to see things straight. And worried over Dad and the baby and all." She tried to smile, but the bright gaiety was gone, and her tilted snub nose was less proud and perky.

"Your Dad'll be all right when he gets over Jord," said Nick Santell. He was scowling and restless, impatient to be off to war, his blue eyes recklessly alight and his lean jaws set. A slim whiplash figure of medium height, Nick was a fighting man, leather-tough, rash and headstrong, proud and rebellious. "Rupe needs me, Mellie. I know I can't take Jord's place with him, but I can help some."

Melora looked at his cocked auburn head and keen, sharp-featured profile with love and pride. She was glad he was a man among men like the Maitlands, glad that her father and brothers had liked and approved of Nick Santell, where they had been either critical or contemptuous of the other boys she was interested in. Once she had hoped to get a man as big and good-looking and casually charming as Jord or Rupe, but when she met the wiry, intense Nick, she knew he was the one for her. At times Nick was difficult— rough, high-strung and profane but he was all man, Melora wouldn't have had him any different. Nick Santell was small only in stature.

"Everybody's goin' this time, Mellie," said Nick. "You wouldn't want me skulkin' back here, danglin' on your apron strings."

She laughed with delight at the absurdity of such a notion. "You aren't exactly the apron-string type, Red-head," she said fondly. "I know you've got to go, Nicky. Just try and be a little careful and take care of yourself as well as Rupert."

Nick Santell grinned. "Rupe'd like that, Mel. Me takin' care of him."

"Well, you can do it," Melora declared stoutly. "Jord and Rupe always said you were the best man they knew to have along in a tight spot."

Nick laughed and threw his arm around her shoulders. "Yeah, I was quite a he-man in my time. Until a yellah-haired gal with laughin' blue eyes and a funny little nose came sashayin' along and ruined my life. I never saw that ball-and-chain, Mellie, until you had it ironed onto my leg!"

Melora swung around to face him, her arms gripping his lean waist, and their lips met in a long, hard kiss. It was Nick who broke away, his mind on the battle ahead, too keyed-up to lose himself in her embrace. They sat down on the mossy bank and watched the water ripple and froth lacy-white around the rocks in the creek.

"What do you think of Karen Hessler, Nick?" Melora asked.

"Not much—right now. But she's liable to be quite a woman when she grows up and steadies down. I think she's in love with Rupe, but he don't know it or won't believe it, or somethin'."

"Then she wasn't in love with Jord?"

"Not really, I guess. Maybe she thought a lot of him, like everybody did, but it wasn't love. She's still flighty and finicky, like all them Southern belles."

"Have you known a lot of them, Nicky?"

"No more'n I could count on the fingers of both hands," Nick Santell said soberly.

Melora smiled and nestled against him. The smell of peach blossoms and sweet grass was fragrant on the evening breeze. The moon was rising in red-gold glory, and the stars were sparkling bright and sharp as diamonds in the darkening azure of the heavens. "I hope you aren't gone long, Nick," murmured Melora, rubbing her cheek against his strong shoulder.

"It won't take long, Mellie. And you folks'll be safe enough here. The slavers are goin' to be too busy holdin' Trayborough to do any outside raidin'. And old Poke could get up out of bed and fight, if he had to."

"I'm not worried about us, Nick. Hester Lambert and I can handle guns, too, you know."

"Well, don't worry about Rupe and me, either." Nick Santell stood up, stretching and sighing. "Time we got started, Mellie. Come on up to the house."

"You can't wait, can you, Nicky?" she said, with a rueful shake of her blonde head. "You go ahead, I'll be up in a minute." She watched him move away with brisk sure strides, a keen slender blade of a man with head high and quizzically cocked.

Melora's eyes filled slowly and brimmed over. She had to be alone for this moment, to weep a little for Jord and all the other dead, and for Nick and Rupert who might be going out to die. For her father and Poke Vetter lying wounded. For her dead mother and her unborn baby, and for herself.

Chapter 9

Campfires bloomed ruddily along Mulehead Flats, where Bassett's Brigade was in bivouac, north of Trayborough. The Cygne and Little Muley united here to form the Big Muley, which flowed south through the town and on toward its junction with the Arkansas River. Sentries were posted, horses grazed on picket lines and in rope corrals, and men lounged at ease about the fires. The ranks of this motley army were swollen by Yankee sympathizers from adjacent territories, husky corn-fed farmers from Nebraska and Iowa, lean tough riders from as far away as the Dakotas. Tales of the atrocities in Trayborough had brought them here bent on vengeance.

In the headquarter's tent, broad, rugged, rock-jawed Reef Bassett had donned his faded army uniform and was Major Bassett again. And trim, neat, bony-faced Henry Holdcroft had dug out his rusty moth-eaten blues and become Captain Holdcroft once more. The brass and the gilt braid were tarnished green, but the men's eyes and brains were as sharp as their sabers, their bodies as fit and well-kept as their guns. Some volunteers wore odds and ends of various uniforms, but most of the men were in the usual working clothes of farmers and riders, teamsters and lumbermen, storekeepers, miners and drifters.

Trayborough had been under siege for three days now, with no full-scale offensive attempted as yet. Along with Bassett's Brigade, two other attacking forces were encamped outside the town. McFeeters and his Missourian Free Staters on the east, Furlong and his mountain men from Colorado on the west. The turnout was far better than Reef Bassett had dared hope for, giving the Northerners a superiority in numbers that should more than offset Atchinson's entrenched defensive position with its stone blockhouses and cannon. According to rumor, some of the slavers were still engaged in a prolonged orgy of debauchery, which further weakened the defenders' cause. Once the three-pronged assault was launched in earnest, it appeared fairly certain that Trayborough would fall. But the price, as in all offensive maneuvers, would be high and dear.

In camp and on patrol, Rupe Maitland had been silent and brooding most of the time, with Nick Santell in constant attendance, and True Lambert and the Syberts with them as much as possible. They all fretted against the waiting and delay, thinking of neglected chores and the strain and hardship inflicted on the womenfolk at home.

This night, scouts had just brought in a group of wretched women they had found wandering, dazed and exhausted, in the woods. Girls from the dance halls and honky-tonks, and girls from good Abolitionist families, fleeing from the drunken violence of Atchinson's guerrillas.

Nick Santell and young Lem Sybert went with most of the others for a look at the pathetic creatures, but Rupe Maitland remained lying on his back at the rim of the firelight, head on his saddle, pipe in teeth, eyes staring at the star-jeweled night-blue sky. Nick and Lem came back after an interval, snarling and cursing. "My God, what they did to them women!" Nick said. "About twelve of 'em, half-starved, dresses tattered, beat up, too. Those dirty, rotten devils!"

It didn't seem to affect Rupe Maitland. Nothing touched him any more. "When we goin' in after them?" he asked. All that interested him was striking at the slavers, getting Early Hessler and the rest under his guns.

"In the mornin', the word just came around," Nick Santell said grimly. "We're movin' out at four o'clock, Rupe."

"Good," Rupe said with satisfaction. "It's about time."

He didn't know much about the overall strategy, except that all three forces would move simultaneously.

McFeeters and Furlong, in from the east and west, would cover the southern flank, while Bassett hit down the river from the north. The Big Muley, still high and floating with driftwood from the spring rains, would afford passage for a raft load of dynamiters disguised under brush and timber. Rupe Maitland was in charge of a detail of sharpshooters, armed with repeaters like his Henry, assigned to cover a squad of mounted dynamiters. After the explosives were hurled in, it would simply be a cavalry charge, with men on foot mopping up in the rear, or so he imagined. That was about the best Bassett and Holdcroft could do with these untrained, undisciplined troops that had seen only three days' service in the field. It should be good enough to sweep the guerrillas out of Trayborough, at any rate.

Rupe hoped the Hessler and Carrick crews hadn't fled when they saw the opposition growing bigger and stronger. Those were the ones he wanted—Clay and Early Hessler, Chance Carrick and Asa Sporn, Huber Northrup and Elwood Kivett.

Nick Santell, with a borrowed repeating rifle, was in Rupe's detachment of sharpshooters, while Lem Sybert and True Lambert were with that dynamiting unit, and fat Sam Sybert was going along as a horse-holder. With time so restricted, Bassett and Holdcroft deemed it advisable to leave the recruits in their own groups, as far as possible. Men familiar with one another should work and get along better together, in most instances. The word was passed for squad leaders to report to headquarters, and Rupe Maitland got up and joined the men straggling in that direction to receive their final instructions.

An hour later, back at the cook fire, Rupe called his crew together and relayed the necessary orders to them as they squatted about drinking coffee from tin cups and smoking, quiet and thoughtful on the eve of battle. Within another hour Rupe was sleeping in his blankets, awaking as quick and alert as usual when Nick touched his shoulder, thinking at first it was time to move out. But the Big Dipper told him it wasn't yet midnight, and Nick said, "Somebody to see you beyond the outpost. The guard here just came in, Rupe."

"Who is it, Nick?"

"A woman on horseback. A redheaded woman, he says."

Rupe Maitland sighed and crawled out of the blankets, fully dressed except for his brush jacket, hat and gun belt. "How'd she ever get out here?" he wondered aloud, pulling on jacket and hat, buckling the double-holstered belt he was now using to carry Jord's Remington along with his Colt. He didn't particularly want to see Dodie Deneen, or anyone else, for that matter. Tapering up and lighting a cigarette, he followed the squat gray-whiskered sentry toward the perimeter of the bivouac. He recognized the picket as old Plosser, the hermitlike character, who last Saturday had warned Nick and Rupe that Carrick's outfit was ahead of them on the road to the farm.

"Gal must be crazier'n a coot, skyhootin' around in the middle of the night. Almost put a slug into her myself before I saw that red hair ablowin' and realized she was a female critter." Plosser winked and grimaced. "A right purty one too, son."

At the outpost Plosser rejoined his fellow sentry, and Rupe walked on toward where Dodie was waiting beside one of the Hessler's sleek rangy horses. Her visit puzzled and irked him. One thing he had enjoyed about this military interlude was the absence of women. She must be like one of the family now, to be riding a Hessler thoroughbred around at midnight. Either that, or she'd stolen the mount.

"You could get shot, Dodie, ridin' this country at night," he said.

"Don't be mad at me, Rupe. I had to see you—just for a minute." Her face looked thinner and harder but was unmarked. The scars Karen had mentioned must be on her back. She went on, laughing: "Besides, after you're flogged in public, shootin' ain't so bad."

"Are you—all right, Dodie?"

"Sure, I'm fine. Scarred up some, but it don't show."

"Still at Hessler Hall?"

"Yeah, Karen's been wonderful to me, Rupe," said

Dodie Deneen. "They've all treated me nice there. Of course the old man and Early tried to get a little fresh on the sly, but they didn't get rough or anythin'. The Hesslers act like gentlemen, whatever else they may be."

"Well, I'm glad you like them," Rupe said dryly, "and your new home."

"I was afraid you'd be this way, Rupe," she said sadly. "You—you blame me for—for what happened to Jord, don't you?" Her husky voice was uneven and shaky.

"I don't want to talk about it, Dodie. What did you want of me?"

"Just to see you, Rupe," she said earnestly, "to tell you how sorry and miserable I've been. I—I love you, Rupe. I can't help it, even if you're tryin' to break with me."

Rupert shook his head irritably. "We've got a war to fight."

"Don't I know it? I had a taste of it myself, Rupe." Her laugh was harsh and cynical. "But they didn't break me. I would've died first. I'll never be anybody's but yours, Rupe." She moved closer, eyes and lips lifted and expectant, her body yearning toward him, but Rupe felt indifferent, cold and hard as granite, almost repelled. He couldn't look at her, or even think of her, without thinking of Jord dying in his arms in that sunny crowded plaza before Gunnarsson's Saloon.

"I'm sorry, Dodie, but I've got to get back," Rupe said softly. "Maybe, after this is all over—"

"No, I know you're through, Rupe," she said bitterly. "I knew it last Saturday, or I was afraid of it. That's why I rode out here tonight, to find out for sure." Dodie laughed with self-mockery. "Well, I found out, didn't I? Go on back and play soldier, Rupe. Women are the damnedest fools! That makes two of us in love with you, and you want neither of us."

"Two of you?"

"Yes, Karen's as foolish as I am. In one respect, anyway."

"She's always in love," Rupe said wearily. "An old Southern custom. It never goes very deep or serious."

"And a woman like *me* couldn't really love anybody, of course."

"I didn't say that, Dodie."

Dodie Deneen made a sweeping gesture and picked up the grounded reins. "You might as well have, Rupe. Sorry I bothered you, soldier. Go on back to your bobtailed army, and—" Her voice choked and died away, her mouth twisted with emotion.

Rupe stepped forward then, but Dodie wheeled, her dark cloak flying out behind her, and flinging herself into the saddle she rode away at a gallop, her hair streaming back in the moonlight, the sound of hoofs lessening with distance.

Rupe Maitland walked slowly back past the smirking sentries into the restless slumbering camp, wishing he had been kinder to Dodie, regretting his loss of feeling for her. But since Jord's death, no one seemed to matter much to him. The only people he cared about were Dad and Melora and Nick, and to a lesser degree Poke Vetter, the Lamberts and the Syberts. Cut off from the rest of the world, isolated from humanity in general, he was becoming steeled and shaped into a hard, sharp instrument of revenge, as single-purposed and ruthless as a saber.

Back in his blankets, it was difficult for Rupe to sleep again, and after he finally did drift off, his slumber was fitful, torn and broken by dreams. When Nick Santell roused him once more, it seemed as if he hadn't slept a wink. As always on waking now, Rupe's first thought was of his dead brother and wounded father; his second, of the Hesslers and the war at hand.

This time the alarm was general and the entire camp was roused to prepare for the assault on Trayborough.

Hessler Hall was in darkness except for the master's study, silent save for the sentry calls and usual sounds from the men bivouacked about the grounds and outbuildings. The most substantial stronghold in the town limits, the manor was the key point in the eastern line of defense, and Clay Hessler had seen to it that ample barricades and breastworks were thrown up around the estate with adequate forces to man them. In the beginning he had doubted that the Free Staters ever would attack Trayborough, but now with all those reinforcements out there, a Northern onslaught was obviously coming. And Hessler wasn't at all certain that the garrison could hold out against superior numbers.

He had little faith in Atchinson, who was more a butcher than a military leader, and the so-called army Atchinson had brought was mostly a ragtag riffraff lot, bent on drunken carousing and looting rather than on fighting. Some of them were still half-drunk and shaken from the orgy that had started as soon as they took the town. Their brutal abuses had failed to stir Clay Hessler in the least, for he had neither sympathy nor tolerance for people in the mass. But the lack of discipline and fighting qualities of Atchinson's horde disgusted him profoundly.

Moving restlessly about the elegant paneled room, Clay Hessler poured himself another glass of brandy, inhaling its aroma and admiring its clear golden color against the slow flames in the great stone fireplace. The walls were lined with books and hung with paintings and ancestral portraits. A gunrack occupied one corner, a collection of swords another. Near the massive mahogany desk was a well-stocked liquor cabinet, with gleaming bottles of odd shapes and many colors. Puffing a long thin cigar and sipping his brandy, Clay Hessler paced the richly carpeted hardwood, fully at home and in harmony with this atmosphere of leisurely gracious living.

In his late forties, Clay stood six-two and was still straight as a lance, lean, sleek-muscled and fit, priding himself in being taller than his son Early. He had a finely shaped, high-held head, the gray streaks in the crisp dark hair giving him a distinguished look. His refined aquiline-nosed features were as truly aristocratic as his tall graceful figure, and his tasteful gray broadcloth draped him with easy perfection. He had the appearance and effortless movements of some lithe predatory animal, and he was equally ruthless.

Clay Hessler was as proud and selfish and egocentric as a man can be. Possessively proud of his son and daughter for their ornamental value, he had no interest in them as individuals and human beings—the same attitude he had toward his beautiful estranged wife and his favorite quarter horses. In a lurid checkered career that afforded many grounds for remorse, Clay was ashamed of only two things, and those but secretly. The fact that Deborah, his wife, had deserted him for a flashy, low-bred New Orleans gambler. And his own conduct in that final duel with Tod Ballister, which had occasioned his hasty departure from Georgia.

The latter had caused Clay to be hypercritical and furious about the manner in which his son Early had killed Jordan Maitland. He had given the boy a merciless tongue-lashing: "If you aren't up to facing a man fairly, for the love of God don't be fool enough to challenge him!" Clay had said, with cruel, biting scorn. "In battle, it's permissible to kill by any means, fair or foul, but in a private affair a man—if he has any honor and integrity in him—fights fair and clean, like a gentleman. You lost your nerve, Early, and turned coward; you waited until Jord unbuckled his belt and then shot him while he was helpless. That's nothing but murder, boy! You might as well have shot him in the back!" Clay had gone on and on for a solid hour, with Early standing there, taut-lipped and white-faced in silent misery.

The fact was that Clay himself had been guilty of a similar breach in his meeting with Tod Ballister. In previous affairs of honor, frequent and unavoidable in the South of that era, Clay Hessler had conducted himself with a courage, dignity and skill that won him considerable esteem. But he had always been unadmittedly afraid of Tod Ballister, and when they faced one another with pistols that morning on the bank of the Chattahoochee, Clay had yielded to fear and fired before the signal was given.

Dismissing this unpleasant memory now, Clay Hessler drained and refilled his glass, and listened intently at the back window for the returning hoofbeats of the horse he had let Dodie Deneen take tonight. The thought occurred that she might not come back at all, in spite of the care he had exercised to treat her with utmost courtesy and generous consideration. That horse was worth a lot of money, and Dodie was undoubtedly still in love with Rupert Maitland. Why should she return to a faction that had striped her beautiful back with a whiplash before hundreds of drunken, jeering men? But Clay's confidence— partially renewed by the brandy—in his own charm reassured him that Dodie would come back, and when she did, he'd see that she no longer spurned him.

The red-haired, green-eyed girl fired the desire that was never far below the polished surface of Clay Hessler. He had wanted her for a long time, but unlike other saloon entertainers, Dodie Deneen was unimpressed by his wealth and power, his fine looks and courtly manners. It was common gossip that, for her, it had been love at first sight when she met Rupe Maitland, two years ago, and Dodie was a one-man girl, except for dancing partners in the Redwing. Her fighting spirit and fiery courage, after shooting down one of Atchinson's rapacious officers, made her all the more desirable to Clay Hessler.

He dwelt on the Maitlands with grudging respect for a moment. For Yankees, they were a family of some quality, Clay confessed. A bit crude and uncouth like all Northerners, but Frank Maitland and the rest had an innate dignity, pleasant, winning ways, a quiet assurance and natural charm that bespoke fine blood and breeding. There were bound to be some genteel folk north of Mason and Dixon's Line, Clay Hessler supposed, and to him the Maitlands exemplified his higher type of Yankee, the rather dubious and hybrid aristocracy of New England. Not to be compared, in any sense, with the blooded aristocrats of the Southland.

Clay regretted somewhat that Early had killed young Jordan Maitland, particularly so because the method reminded him of his own cowardice in the Ballister case, and indicated that Early had a similar inherent flaw. It infuriated Clay to see any sign of weakness reproduced in his son, and parental guilt made him act doubly contemptuous of the boy, widening the breach already between them.

At one time Clay Hessler almost hoped that Karen

would marry a Maitland, first Rupe and then Jord, and he was certain she could have led either of them to the altar if she hadn't persisted in playing the fickle, flirtatious, easy-to-court but hard-to-win spoiled beauty, like any empty-headed Southern coquette. Since her mother's deficiencies had been exposed to the world, Clay looked and feared for the worst in Karen, positive that she would reflect Deborah's lack of stability and character. He thought men like Rupe and Jord Maitland might have kept her in line, where others could not. As much as he hated Yankees, Clay Hessler was honest enough to admit that the Maitlands stood high above the other young men of the Osawatomie country. But all that was over the dam and finished now, with Jord dead and Rupe sworn to kill Early on sight.

Clay enjoyed the company of Elwood Kivett and Huber Northrup, gay, witty young blades from the easy, gracious Southern world he missed so much. But they were professional adventurers, rakehells and libertines, and he'd never permit Karen to marry the likes of them. As for lank Chance Carrick and slim, fiery Asa Sporn, he tolerated them only as hired gunfighters, but Clay Hessler wouldn't take a drink with them nor allow Karen to associate with the wild, hard-bitten Texans. If he lived through this, Clay reflected, and saved the fortune he had recently transferred here from the bank, he would send Karen somewhere in the South—not Georgia, however—and she could find a suitable husband there.

Finding his glass empty, Clay Hessler filled it again, his thoughts reverting to Dodie Deneen with impatience. He glanced at his watch. It was nearly two o'clock. She should be back by now, if she was coming at all. Perhaps she and Rupe were laughing at him this minute, happy in one another's arms, idly figuring how much cash Dodie could realize from the thoroughbred she had borrowed. Well, lending her the horse for the midnight excursion and waiting up for her return was a way Clay had conceived of seeing her alone, unknown to Karen and Early and the rest of the emergency-filled household. If it worked, all right. If it didn't, nothing was lost but a good horse and a few hours' sleep. And a romance Clay had impatiently wanted to bring to fruition.

He was finishing his drink when he heard the faint clip-clop of hoofs, the challenge of a sentry, and then the hoofs chopping closer in the night. Clay Hessler turned down the lamps, then stepped out into the dim hallway and waited by the door through which Dodie Deneen must enter, his pulse and breath quickening, his mouth and throat dry.

The door opened with quiet care, and Dodie started and stiffened at the sight of the tall, smiling man, the light in his dark eyes belying the pleasant curve of his handsome mouth. "I was worred about you, Dodie," said Clay Hessler, in soft, cultured tones. "I couldn't sleep. Was your mission successful? Did everything go satisfactorily?"

Dodie Deneen nodded silently, more afraid now than she had been in the rough hands of Atchinson's drunken brutes.

"Will you join me in a nightcap?"

"No, thanks. I'm too tired." She raised an uncertain hand to her fiery wind-blown hair.

Clay's hand caught her other wrist in a steel grip. "I think you'd better have a drink with me, Dodie." With steady, relentless strength he drew her into his study and closed the door. "It'll be much better if you don't try to struggle or scream."

Dodie's green eyes and full lips were contemptuous. "What if I do fight and yell?"

"In the first place, it won't do any good. No one will come to your rescue. Nobody will dare to interfere. In the second, I will feel forced to knock you unconscious. Please don't make me do that, Dodie."

She studied him with cool disdain. "All your pride must be on the surface, mister. Inside you haven't even got self-respect. You've got a son and daughter as old as I am, Hessler. They ought to be real proud of a father like you!"

"You're wasting your breath and my time." Clay smiled, unperturbed by her sarcasm. "Do you want a drink, Dodie?"

Dodie Deneen shrugged. "Well, I've been beaten

about all I care to stand—for a while. Go ahead, Southern gentleman, get the drinks."

As he moved away from her, Clay Hessler caught the flickering motion of her hand beneath the blue cloak, and knew instinctively that Dodie had a pistol there, and that she would use it. Wheeling swiftly back and drawing from his shoulder holster, Clay Hessler rapped his gun barrel sharply across the glimmering red-gold of her head. Gasping and going limp on sagging knees, Dodie would have fallen to the floor if Clay hadn't caught her with strong expert arms. His patrician features showing not the slightest emotion but for a strange flickering of his eyes, Clay Hessler carried the girl toward a secret door concealed in the polished walnut paneling near the open fireplace.

Chapter 10

Bassett's Brigade was on the move in the early morning blackness, fogged and chill with gray vapors swirling in from the Cygne and Little Muley, making wraiths of the horses and men. After a quick cold breakfast, shivering and swearing volunteers saddled up and loaded gear with stiff numb fingers, metal freezing to the touch and leather itself rigid with cold. Stumbling and blundering about in the damp gloom, the ranks finally formed, with much jostling confusion and sullen cursing, into some semblance of order. Now the wide sprawling columns were moving off Mulehead Flats and down the valley toward Trayborough, while from somewhere to the west Furlong was bringing up his Colorado mountaineers, and from the east McFeeters closed in with his Missourians.

Rupe Maitland rode at the head of his riflemen, frost-stiffened saddle leather creaking, equipment jangling and clinking, breaths pluming out white in the darkness. Rupe and his crew wore extra bandoleers of shells slung across the shoulder and carried two handguns, along with the booted carbines and the sabers that had been issued to riders in the forward ranks. Gradually as the saddles warmed, blood began to circulate more freely, muscles limbered up, and the men came fully awake and alive.

After an hour of slow marching, everything was moving smoother and easier, spirit and morale were rising, and Trayborough was before them but still hidden. Wan gray light showed on the eastern horizon, the darkness slowly starting to filter away and fade into murky grayness, the mists rising and spreading denser than ever. The turf underfoot was soggy and rimmed with dew, and faces and hands were wet from the moisture-laden haze in the air. Progress grew even slower as they neared striking distance. All along the front ranks, squads of the dynamite detail nerved themselves for an effort that verged on the suicidal, with groups of Rupe's riflemen getting ready to cover them.

The primary objective before Rupe Maitland's section, still invisible in the shifting fog and darkness, was the old stone tannery that had been converted into a blockhouse by the defenders, with trenches and earthworks in front of it. A focal point in the northern defense line, it would be a difficult spot to break through.

Vandiveer, in command of the demolition unit ahead of Rupert, raised his arm to halt the column, and Rupe passed the signal back. That band of light was widening on the eastern skyline, streaked with pale green and lavender and lemon color, as darkness ebbed away, leaving the earth in misted neutral dimness. Vandiveer's men dismounted and prepared to move forward on foot, the horse-holders taking their mounts. Rupe Maitland lifted the Henry from its boot and swung down; Nick Santell and the others followed suit, leaving their horses with the holders and fanning into position to cover the initial advance.

The large stone building and parts of the town could be seen now, ghostly and unreal through the weaving vapors. True Lambert and Lemuel Sybert waved cheerfully back at Rupe as they started forward, and behind him Rupe heard old Sam Sybert swearing or praying softly as he held his bunch of horses. Vandiveer's detail was soon swallowed up in the fog, and Rupe and his followers waited in a breathless hush, senses sharpened and nerves on edge. If those men were spotted before they got in close enough to hurl their charges, they'd all be shot down or blown up with their own explosives, thus losing the surprise element and its vital advantages. Time passed, the colors brightened in the east, the whole sky lightened shade by shade, and the first rays of dawn fingered the gray landscape.

It was painful waiting for the enemy guns to break out.

Rupe accepted the offer of Nick's tobacco plug and bit off a generous chew, welcoming the tang and the activity of his jaws. Shells levered in and rifles ready, the men peered into the hazy curtain and waited. Then the first blasts shattered the stillness, rocked the earth, and illuminated the earthworks and the sooty stone walls of the tannery. There was a tremendous explosion from the Big Muley River, and other roaring concussions along the northern outskirts. The racket of slaver gunfire started up, thin and brittle under the thundering explosives, and men came running back up the misted slope as Rupe and his riflemen hammered shots over their heads into the enemy position.

They fired until their repeaters were spent, and all of Vandiveer's dynamiters who had survived were back, clambering into saddles and clawing out handguns and sabers. Reloading quickly and yelling, "Mount up! Mount up and move forward!" Rupe Maitland swung into the leather, booted the Henry, and circled his raw-boned bay gelding until the others were ready for the charge. The brass scream of bugles echoed along the line, and the attack rolled forward. Reins in teeth, Rupe held Jord's Remington in his left hand, the saber in the right, and drove forward at the gallop with thighs clinging and body rocking easily to the powerful reaching strides of the big bay.

Rupe glimpsed a bulky form in the grass as he hurtled past, and it looked like Lem Sybert, but he couldn't be certain. Whoever it was, there was no life left there. Rupe feared that Lem was gone, for he hadn't seen the chunky moon-faced boy come back with the other dynamiters, although he had witnessed with relief the return of True Lambert. After that it was one long hideous nightmare to Rupe Maitland.

They cleared the breastworks and hurdled a trench, with pistols blazing and sabers slashing and bullets searing all about them. Horses and men went down screaming on either side, but Rupe and Nick went rocketing onward, yelling their thoats raw without even knowing it. The tannery was partly demolished, but muzzle flames were still licking out from some of the windows. No time to stop and clean out that nest; the men behind would have to do that. They swept past the stone building with its blasted walls agape and guns snarling at them. Rupe shot down a man in a ruined doorway, and Nick sabered another as he broke and ran before them. They surged on toward the middle of the settlement, head-on into a deadly lashing crossfire that spilled horses and riders in thrashing tangled heaps. Too hot to go through there. It seemed as if enemy rifles were roaring from every window in every house.

Cavalry couldn't go into that scourging crosswhip of fire and lead without eighty percent casualties. Nothing to do now but pull back and dismount, sling the sabers and go to the carbines, spread out and do some shooting of their own, smoke them out of one house after another. Slow, maddening, nerve-racking work. Sniping at muzzle flashes, crawling through rubble, flattening out in filthy alleys, skulking across littered backyards. Swearing and sweating and firing away, as the sun rose bloodred and the slavers fell stubbornly back from one building to the next.

Pinned down behind the sagging splintered wreckage of a riddled back porch, Rupe Maitland and Nick Santell grinned wryly at one another with powder-grimed, sweat-varnished faces. "At this rate we won't get a drink in Gunnarsson's until afternoon," Rupe complained.

"Hell, there ain't any whiskey left in this town," Nick said. "Atchinson's hogs swilled it all down."

"There'll be some at Hessler Hall," Rupe said.

"I wouldn't know about that," Nick answered. "Right now I'd rather have beer than anythin' else. About a gallon of it, nice and cold."

"Shut up!" groaned Rupe. "And give me another chew of that nice cold tobacco of yours." But the slavers retreated faster as more Free Staters poured into the embattled town and the pressure increased remorselessly on the defenders. It was a long, slow, bloody forenoon of street-fighting, but the spearhead of Bassett's Brigade was almost in to the central square by twelve o'clock. On the west, Furlong's force had driven in through the slums as far as the Redwing, just off the plaza. But things hadn't gone so well in the east. McFeeters, unable even to make a dent in the defensive lines around Hessler Hall, had split his company widely to the south and north, and made little headway anywhere.

That left the slaver line intact from the square to the Hessler mansion on the eastern rim of town. Their two strongholds in the center of the community were Gunnarsson's long stone-block saloon and the brick bank building. Many previously burned wooden structures were nothing but charred cellar holes, and others were blazing up now and adding to the wicked midday heat. As this heat increased, the stench of the dead became unbearable, and the screams of the wounded rose and echoed everywhere in that flaming, reeking, smoke-shrouded charnel house of a town.

There proved to be less resistance in the square than they had anticipated, as most of the slavers seemed to have had a stomachful of slaughter and were intent on falling back to Hessler Hall, where Clay Hessler and Atchinson and Carrick had the best Southern troops, the strongest defense lines, and the two cannons. The Free Staters fought their way into the plaza at one-twenty in the afternoon and knew then that the climax of the battle would come at the Hessler home.

Two dead slavers were half-submerged in the watering trough at the center of the square, with three others tumbled in ragged bloody heaps about its base. Thirst-crazed Yankees, who had either emptied or mislaid their canteens, hauled the corpses from the stone tub and bent to gulp the stained water before it had time to refresh itself from the constant-running spout. Others waited until the water was clean and filled their canteens.

Reef Bassett and Henry Holdcroft called for the horses to be brought up and volunteers for a cavalry charge on Hessler Hall. "They're beaten men," Bassett announced in his deep-toned voice. "If we hit them full force now, they'll never stand against us. Let's get this bloody business over so we can go home to our families and our work!"

A hoarse cheer went up from the sun-dazzled square,

and Rupe Maitland smiled thinly at Santell. It was obvious that they'd get their volunteers—almost every man that was still able to ride and fight. They all wanted to finish it up as soon as possible.

Rupe was sick and tired to the bone of the whole show, appalled by the waste of life, the horrible suffering, the murderous fury of men in battle. But he would go on, because there was nothing else to do. A man had to live up to his own and his comrades' conception of him, a matter of self-respect more than anything else. Leaning against the bleached boards of a caved-in awning, Rupe shaped and lighted a cigarette, inhaling against the gagging green smell of putrefying flesh. Dead horses and men, obscenely bloated, lay crumpled around the square, and more-recently slain Southerners hung from windows, blocked doorways, and huddled beneath jagged broken awnings. Flies swarmed in thick buzzing clouds, and vultures flapped evilly overhead. The debris of combat was everywhere: broken glass, splintered wood, firearms and swords, pieces of clothing and equipment, wastepaper and bloody rags—and the stinking dead.

Rupe Maitland retched and revolted against all of it, yet there was a mild inner satisfaction in having come through the fiery test. He had stood it better than he would have before Jord's death, he thought, for life meant less to Rupe now and risking it was easier. His worst fear was of being wounded, blinded, mutilated, crippled for life. Death, in comparison to that, would be welcome. Just so it came quick, even if there was no dignity nor human decency in this kind of death.

Sam Sybert, portly and sweat-soaked, brought their horses in from the back street, gnawing frenetically at his powder-blackened gray mustache. "They kilt Lem, god-damn them," he mumbled. "Dead before it even started, Lemuel was. I dunno what I'm goin' to tell his ma. She ain't goin' to be fit to live with after this."

"We had to fight 'em, Sam," said Rupe Maitland gently. "They'd have killed and burned us all in our own homes. Lem's saved a lot of good lives by givin' up his own here. You tell Abigail that."

Sybert nodded gratefully. "Well, I hope it does some good, Rupe. Hate to think it was purely wasted. True's back there with a busted leg, boys. Horse shot down and True didn't get clear. Them doctors Reef and Henry brung in are workin' like slaves, but they can't take care of all them wounded."

"True's out of it, then," Rupe said. "At least he'll live, Sam."

"Yeah, he wanted me to come back, Rupe. So I'm goin' to do what I can. Too old and fat to bog down a horse in any cavalry charge." Sam Sybert plodded away with bowed head and slumped shoulders.

Reef Bassett's bull-bellowing voice rang out over the plaza: "All right, men, form up! In your same squads as near as you can. Come on, we're movin' out! . . . That's better, that's fine, boys. Prepare to mount! Mount!"

They swung into sun-warmed leather with a concerted smash, a pretty fair irregular cavalry considering their lack of experience.

"By fours—Ho!"

They filed after the blue-shirted backs of broad Reef Bassett and thin Henry Holdcroft, out of the open square toward the eastern end of Trayborough. Past more dead men and animals, more burned-out houses, some still flaming, toward Hessler Hall on its eminent terraced lawns.

The white picket fence that surrounded the estate was hidden by rude breastworks of dirt and rock and timber. The green lawns were dug with trenches, piled with barricades, chopped into brown muck by hoofs and boots and wheels. The colonnaded manor itself stood proud and serene as ever, untouched except for broken windows and bullet-scarred walls. The outbuildings looked neat and secure still, with men massed about them and the cannon set up at the crest of the rise.

"That ain't no easy nut to crack," a man said. "We oughta hold off until night and hit 'em in the dark."

"To hell with that!" said another. "I got a sick woman and cows to milk at home."

Nick Santell's bright blue eyes flicked at Rupe. "It looks kinda tough, Rupe. It looks pretty solid."

"I don't think they'll hold, Nick. It takes real troopers to stand against a full head-on charge. They'll break and run under it."

"What about the cannon?"

Rupe grinned, licking his dry, chapped lips with tobacco juice. "They don't look like much. Maybe kill more of their own men than ours."

The conflict had taken on a more personal aspect for Rupe Maitland at this point. Young Early Hessler and his father Clay were up there. So were Butcher Atchinson and Chance Carrick. Likewise Asa Sporn and Elwood Kivett and Huber Northrup—the ones he wanted to get at. It was worth a ride into cannon, gun muzzles and the flaming jaws of hell itself to get a crack at those murderers. But it was bound to cost the Free Staters a lot of casualties.

Bassett and Holdcroft were spreading their followers out among the smoking battered houses and ruins below the slaver defenses on the north, making ready for a direct frontal assault from there. Furlong was gathering his mountain men on the western flank to drive in on that side, while McFeeters, his force not strong enough to attack, was supposed to fight a holding action in the east and south, thus completing the encirclement of Hessler Hall. But Reef Bassett was worried about McFeeters and his Missouri farmers. It showed in the major's craggy red face and stormy sunken eyes.

Rupe Maitland wondered if Karen Hessler and Dodie Deneen were still up there in the great fieldstone mansion. They must be, unless Clay Hessler had come to see their position as untenable and pulled out with his family and friends.

The command came at last: "Forward, ho!" and trumpets shrilled into a high brassy scream. It was a relief to be moving somewhere again, even into the teeth of enemy gunfire. Crowding through backyards, streets and alleys, the charge picked up speed and struck this eastern end of Front Street at a gallop, thundering across it toward the lower earthworks at the foot of the lawn.

Flame lashed out in solid sheets from the barrier,

cutting down horses and riders on all sides of Rupe
Maitland and Nick Santell, but they went on with the rest
in sweeping momentum, straight into the belching fire-
laced smoke of the barricade. Slavers were breaking and
fleeing as the cavalry crashed headlong into the breastworks, ploughing and hurdling over with pistols blaring and
sabers agleam in swift savage arcs. Trampling, shooting and
slashing down defenders in a roaring, hacking red chaos,
they burst the line and hurtled on up the slope in the
furnace glare of afternoon heat.

Heedless of the rifle fire from above, emptying saddles
at every stride, the Yankees stampeded on in a mad torrent,
riding down frantic running men, firing and sabering like
maniacs, driving on past shattered magnolias and down-
trodden rose bushes. A cannon blasted once from the
summit, tearing a terrible swath through the mounted
ranks, dismembering horses and men in a screeching
welter. But the charge went on, the Southern gunners
never having time to reload that piece, shot and cut down
under the hoofs of the onrushing Northerners, dying under
the bite of lead and steel, the stamping hoofs of horses.

Then the first Yankee horsemen to reach the top were
mowed down in turn by blistering fire from Hessler Hall
and the last barricade before it. The others were beaten
back to midslope, Rupe and Nick among them, their blades
crimsoned and dripping, their revolvers spent. Reloading
in the saddle, the heat-shimmering air about them alive
with searching bullets, they re-formed and started another
onslaught, with Reef Bassett up to lead them. Little Henry
Holdcroft lay dead, riddled in a trampled bed of Cherokee
roses, Rupe observed as he galloped by on his lathered bay.
Sanity had long since left Rupe and the rest and the whole
ghastly affair.

This time the slavers met them with a sudden
mounted counterattack of their own, the Southern horses
surging out of the background and over the broad summit,
led by Chance Carrick and Asa Sporn. The two forces
collided head-on with shocking, grinding violence, guns
ablaze and sabers flashing, horses and men thrown in
thrashing, rolling piles on the torn muddied grass.

By sheer chance in the blind melee, Rupe Maitland rode full tilt into Huber Northrup, saber-blades clashing and clanging with sparked fury as their mounts met squarely and reared on the impact. Hilts and guards locked. Northrup was trying to line his left-hand pistol when Rupe gave an explosive wrench that ripped the saber out of Huber's grasp and sent it soaring in a brilliant arc. Fear and horror on his features, Huber Northrup was still trying to level his gun when Rupe's blade slashed his throat. In a vivid geyser of scarlet, Northrup rocked back and floundered earthward.

A gun flared almost in Rupe's face, blinding and searing him as he came around on the bay gelding, and he had a blurred glimpse of Elwood Kivett's sneering saturnine face as he threw down left-handed with Jord's Remington. Before he could trigger, Nick Santell rammed in with his sleek black horse, his dripping red saber striking Elwood Kivett across the head, bowing and bending him, beating him from the saddle facedown against the churned sod, dead under the stomping steel of that insanely vicious dogfight. And then with amazing suddenness, the enemy was routed and in total flight, turning and running all along the line, streaming back in panic past the final barrier and the gray-brown walls of the manor house.

"Come on, boys! We've got 'em now!" bellowed Reef Bassett, rising high and wide in his stirrups and waving a bloody blade overhead. "On to the last damn ditch and Hessler Hall!" But his mount pitched kicking to the ground then, and Reef Bassett was left behind on foot as the charge started.

Rupe and Nick were still riding, vaguely surprised to find themselves still alive and unwounded, save for minor bruises and abrasions. Sweat-plastered and weary in their saddles, shirts in soaked, filthy tatters, sword-arms aching tired, sweat smarting in their eyes, the taste of gunpowder rank in their mouths and throats. The mansion loomed enormous before them, fire flickering from the windows, flame springing out in sheets from that last barricade, death snarling everywhere in the sun-scorched afternoon.

The slavers were still fighting there. They were backed to the wall in a last-ditch stand, pouring their fire into the on-driving Yankee cavalry, howling defiantly as the charge came at them in screeching thunder and the lightning streaks of guns.

Chapter 11

Only a few riders made that first breakthrough, and most of them were shot down after they passed the barrier. The bulk of the attack was halted, scythed down, or whipped back under withering gunfire. But Reef Bassett had caught himself a riderless runaway horse and was in the saddle again, re-forming the scattered decimated ranks and calling up replacements, organizing the Free Staters for another assault. Many of the slavers had had enough, however, and were running to the rear before the Yankees could strike another time.

Rupe Maitland and Nick Santell were among those who broke through, and the only ones to reach the white-pillared porch of Hessler Hall. Nick was hit in the left arm, his horse killed under him. Kicking clear and landing on his feet, Nick caught the tail of Rupe's big bay and was towed on to the front steps, where Rupe reined up and flung himself from the leather. Thrusting his saber into the dirt, Rupe yanked the Henry rifle from its boot and turned to Nick, who was leaning against a white column, his left arm dangling broken and blood-drenched, his thin face drawn and haggard under the black powder smears and glistening sweat.

Behind them the Free Staters were coming on once more, over their own dead this time, and the flight of slavers from the barricade was becoming general. Most of them paid no attention to the two men on the front veranda, but one of the routed Southerners paused to level his rifle. Firing the Henry quickly from his hip, Rupe dropped the man dead across an uprooted magnolia.

"Come on inside, Nicky," said Rupe Maitland, moving to the door and trying it with his left hand, the carbine in the crook of his right elbow. Nick Santell nodded and stumbled after him, a .44 Colt hanging in his right hand. Someone was unlocking the door now, and Rupe lined the Henry waist-high as he stepped back. The door opened narrowly and Dodie Deneen stood there. She was hollow-cheeked, dull-eyed, the sunlight gilding her red hair with fiery gold.

"Any slavers in there?" Rupe asked sharply, wondering what had happened to make her look so desolate and hopeless.

"Not right here, not now," Dodie said lifelessly. "They're all runnin' out, I think. Come in, before you get it in the back."

Rupe motioned Nick in ahead of him, and Rupe's boot was on the threshold when a crushing hammer blow sledged his right side, jolting and turning him around, shoulders against the left-hand door jamb.

Asa Sporn was crouched at the end of the porch, a faint mocking smile on his leathery face, the smoking gun in his right hand coming down into line from the recoil. Rupe tried to jerk the Henry level, but his whole right side felt numb and paralyzed. Unable to lift the rifle barrel, Rupe Maitland hung there on the doorjamb and looked death straight in the face as Asa Sporn took deliberate aim, preparing to pump another slug home. "Right in the gut this time, Rupe," the Texan drawled.

A split second before flame blossomed with a bellowing roar from Asa Sporn's steady hand, Dodie Deneen threw herself forward from the doorway and wheeled in front of Rupe. She shuddered, stiffening, then lurched backward as the bullet smashed her. Catching her in his left arm, Rupe heaved the Henry up and triggered it like a pistol, the recoil racking his wounded side agonizingly. But Asa Sporn had vanished, gone as if he never had been there.

Rupe shouldered the sagging girl toward the entrance,

and then Nick was there to lend his one good hand and help them stagger inside.

The great paneled hallway was dim and quiet after the outer brightness and din, a crystal chandelier sparkling high overhead in the slanting sunbeams from an upper window. They put Dodie on the leather settee against the left wall, across from the magnificent staircase. Rupe sank down beside her, shocked and sick from his own wound as well as from Dodie's sacrifice, and Nick Santell stood swaying before them.

"Is it bad, Dodie?" asked Rupe.

The girl writhed until her red head rested on Rupe's left thigh, the dark stain spreading on her green dress. "I'm dyin', Rupe," she whispered, with a ghost of her old gay smile. "But it's all right—a good thing. Just remember, Rupe—I love you—always. Don't ever—forget—"

A convulsive shudder shook her, twisted the keen gaunted face, and the light went out of those green eyes, the last breath sighed from her slack lips. Dodie Deneen was dead, with her golden-red head on Rupe's knee. Nick snatched a drape off the wall, hauled Dodie clear of Rupe, and tenderly covered her.

"Asa Sporn had me cold, Nick," Rupe said. "Dodie walked into one that was meant for me."

"Well, you got it bad enough yourself, friend."

"How about you?"

Nick Santell snorted. "Busted arm, that's all. Just a damn nuisance. Where the hell is everybody here?"

They could hear the sounds of battle outside and slight stirrings somewhere in the depths of the interior. "Maybe it's just as well if they're gone," Rupe mused. "The shape we're in, Nick."

"Let me look at your side, Rupe."

"Not now; there isn't time." Rupert levered a shell into the chamber, laid the carbine across his knees, and painfully checked his revolvers. Nick locked the front door, drawing his gun again immediately, blue eyes roving and alert.

Footsteps sounded on the stairway above.

Nick's gun hand snapped up, and then fell slowly back.

It was Karen Hessler, descending swiftly as she saw them there, her fine features drawn with anxiety and terror, her dark eyes wide and staring.

"Is that—Dodie?" She pointed at the draped body in horror.

When Rupe nodded in silent response, Karen noticed his bloodsoaked right side. "You're hurt, Rupe! Is it bad?"

"I don't think so."

"Let me see, Rupe."

"It wouldn't be pretty, Karen."

"Don't be a fool!" she cried in exasperation. "I know something about nursing, and I'm not afraid of blood."

"It'll wait," Rupe said. "Where are the men of the house?"

"Gone, or getting ready to go, I guess. Or dead at their windowsills."

"Your father and Early?"

"They're still alive, Rupe," she said, almost with indifference. "Please let me help you. You're losing a lot of blood."

Rupe turned his blond head. "You don't want to help me, Karen. I'm here to kill your brother."

"You're in no condition to kill anyone, Rupe." Nick Santell spoke gravely: "But I am, miss."

"Tell me about Dodie," said Karen Hessler.

"It's a long story," Rupe drawled.

"Yes, and you don't know all of it, either," Karen said with such bitterness that they both stared wonderingly at her.

Bullets were still chewing at the stone walls of the house, and lead shattered the hall window and ripped splinters off the carved woodwork over their heads. An upstairs shot set the fine cut glass chandelier to clinking and brought down a bright spattering of crystals. From the sounds outside, there was still savage fighting along the earthworks.

An abrupt spasm of agonizing pain shook Rupe Maitland. It was so scaldingly intense it almost wrung an involuntary cry of protest from between his clenched teeth. A steaming reddish haze obscured the room, and he fought against giddy faintness, panting hard and sweating in agony. The Henry rifle slid from his knees unnoticed, and Rupe lay back on the couch in anguish and weakness, head arched against the wall, throat corded and breath rasping. With all his will and ebbing power he clung to consciousness, knowing it could not be for long. Feeling the life and strength seep out of him, Rupe wondered if this was the way death came. . . .

Gun butts were hammering at the front door, and Nick Santell whirled, his left arm hanging useless, his Colt in his right fist, eyes watchful and wary. Behind him, at the far end of the corridor, another door opened noiseless and Clay Hessler stepped through, smiling tautly and raising a long-barreled pistol.

Karen cried out just before the gun blasted with a deafening roar that filled the vestibule. Rupert saw this dimly, like something in a bad dream, but he could not move or speak or lift a finger. Tears of helplessness blurred his vision, and a dry sob broke in his parched aching throat.

Driven three tottering steps forward by that shocking impact against his spine, Nick Santell swayed on numbed spraddled legs. Desperately he strove to turn on the attacker, fire back. But his muscles refused to answer, his legs and arms wouldn't work, his body was frozen in paralysis.

"Get him, Rupe!" panted Nick Santell. "Get the slavin' snake for me!" Once more Nick tried to wheel about, but his spine was broken and he couldn't turn or move, except to collapse moaning on the polished hardwood. He went rigid, then limp and loose, his lips moving against the floor as life drained from his broken body.

Clay Hessler stood tall, handsome and distinguished-looking, his black eyes piercing and his mouth scornful. Karen had moved between him and Rupe, and Clay swerved the smoking gun in that direction.

"Stand aside, Karen," he ordered, as the chandelier tinkled overhead and another thin rain of glass flashed floorward. Then, for the first time Clay saw the covered body beside Rupe as a strand of coppery hair caught the light. "What happened to her?" he demanded.

"You might as well have killed her last night," Karen said, cold and contemptuous. "She didn't want to live—"

"Shut up and stand clear, Karen!"

"No, you aren't going to murder him, too," Karen said firmly, protecting Rupe Maitland as he slouched there half-senseless. She flung herself between his long body and the man with the gun. "You'll have to shoot me first!"

"Don't be a goddamned idiot. Get out of the way, girl!"

"Shoot," invited Karen, pressing herself back to shield Rupe. "That's the way the Hesslers kill, isn't it? Go ahead, shoot us both!"

"By God, daughter!" Clay Hessler swore in frustration, and moved toward them with catlike grace.

"Don't call me daughter!" she spat back at him. "Hit me over the head with the gun. That's what you do to girls, isn't it?"

Clay Hessler was reaching out to grasp her shoulder and tear her away from Rupe, when Early shouted from the rear of the house: "Dad! Hurry up, Dad! The Yankees are breakin' through everywhere. We've got to get out of here fast. Come on—the horses are waitin'!"

Clay Hessler paused, frowning and shaking his crisp dark head with its picturesque tinges of gray. Heavy boots tramped the porch, gun butts slammed at the door panels, and hoarse voices yelled in the yard. Window glass broke with a jangled crash. "All right, Karen," said Clay Hessler, "stay with your damned Yankee!" He turned and strode back the way he had come: out of her sight, and out of her life.

Tears flooding her pale cheeks, Karen rose and bent over Rupe Maitland, but he was entirely unconscious now. "You see, Rupe?" she whispered. "It's you, Rupe—it's always been you. It always will be. And I'll take care of you now, Rupert. I'll make you well."

Straightening slowly, Karen Hessler wheeled and walked sadly around the crumpled lifeless form of Nick Santell, where it lay facedown against the floorboards. Then she unlocked and opened the great front door of

Hessler Hall for the weary, bleeding and battle-grimed Northerners.

Half-lying on the leather couch behind her, Rupe Maitland regained consciousness for a fleeting instant. He thought, *I'm dying for sure, but it don't matter much. Everybody—Jord and Dodie and Nick and all the rest. Except for Dad and Melora, I'll be in better company.* Then he drifted back into depthless dark, the perfect peace of oblivion.

For two weeks Rupert Maitland hovered in the border wasteland between life and death, semiconscious and raving with fever and not caring most of the time. It wasn't the wound so much, Doc Kinderness declared, as the fact that Rupe had lost interest in living. The bullet had broken two ribs and lodged in the body, fortunately short of the abdominal cavity. Kinderness had removed the lead before infection could set in, and recovery should have been a matter of course. But apparently Rupe had suffered injuries that went beyond the physical. He didn't seem to care enough to fight his way back to life and health.

Hessler Hall had been converted into a hospital, crowded with the wounded of both sides, where Kinderness and the other doctors and volunteer nurses worked around the clock, in summer heat made hideous by the screams of the wounded and the outside stench of still-unburied dead.

Karen Hessler astonished everyone by taking charge of the nurses and working harder than any of them. In this emergency the Southern belle outdid the hardiest of pioneer women. Karen's tireless strength and rare courage, quiet patience and infinite good cheer, became legendary in Trayborough. Some said she was trying to make up for the evil wrought by her father and brother. Others thought she was doing it mainly for the sake of Rupe Maitland.

"A man never gets too old to be surprised by a woman," Doc Kinderness said, scratching his tousled gray head and rubbing his gaunt seamed cheeks. "I always figured Karen Hessler was a typical Southern coquette, bright and decorative but empty-headed and useless. I used to pity Jord Maitland for falling in love with her, and I always congratulated Rupe for getting wise to her in time. But now I take it all back after what that girl's done for us here. The lives she's saved and the dying hours she's brightened, working twenty-four hours a day and half-dead on her feet herself. Karen Hessler is a great and gallant lady. And she brought Rupe Maitland back to life single-handed. She just *wouldn't* let him die!"

While Doc Kinderness, Karen Hessler and the rest labored to save lives and ease the suffering of hopeless cases, volunteer labor gangs were digging graves and burying the dead and cleaning up the settlement. The surviving slavers, including their leaders, had escaped and fled southward through the breaches left by McFeeters and his Missourians. Atchinson the Butcher, Clay and Early Hessler, Chance Carrick and Asa Sporn had made their getaway. Regrettable, but if they stayed away it was nearly as good as having them dead. The Osawatomie was all Abolitionist now, and Free State families began to drift back to rebuild their homes and business places in Trayborough. A crude new village mushroomed from the bloody ashes of the old, and grew rapidly in the summer sunshine.

When Rupe Maitland emerged from his delirium, he found no immediate incentive to live. Almost everyone he cared about, except Dad and Melora, was dead. Gone were Mom and Jord, Dodie Deneen and Nick Santell; Lem Sybert and Joe Gayle and Eastlach; Henry Holdcroft, the Brownlees, and all the others. It left an empty world that he didn't care to inhabit, particularly since Clay and Early Hessler were out of reach, along with Atchinson and Carrick and Asa Sporn. The ones who most deserved to die were still alive and at large. Tattam, Kivett and Northrup had gone under, but the worst of the crew, so far as anyone knew, were still free and well.

As Rupe became more rational and coherent, Doc Kinderness attempted to rouse him and fan his spirit alive. "Three bullets didn't kill your father, Rupe," he jibed. "Are you going to let just one finish you? Old Poke Vetter's already up and around, a man of his age, and harder hit than you were. And old True Lambert isn't letting a broken leg keep him down, either." But Rupe merely smiled faintly and turned his head on the pillow, refusing to catch fire and flare back at the big doctor, remaining dull and indifferent.

It took Karen and her subtler woman's way to renew Rupe's interest in the world about him. Without ever seeming to preach, she pointed out his father's need of him with Jordan gone, and Melora's dependence on him, since Nick was lost to both her and her unborn child. She mentioned the resilience and courage of the settlers coming back to restore their ruined homes in Trayborough, among them the Eastlach and Gayle families. Life had to go on for the living; their dead would ever be cherished in memory but not as an obsession. A man couldn't let go and quit at the prime age of twenty-seven. A man had to fight, as long as the breath and blood were in him. He owed it to himself, as well as to his loved ones.

Karen didn't say these things directly. Her low, rich voice flowed on, slow and soothing as a lazy meadow stream, and the patterns of meaning appeared like sun-brightened pebbles under the surface. And as Rupe grew more aware and responsive, he came to notice the change, the new maturity in Karen Hessler. Her face had thinned and firmed, her superb bone structure giving it strength and character. Her private ordeal of grief and pain, her daily contact with suffering humanity, had brought out the inner nobility of Karen's nature. There was new depth in her great dark eyes, set at that slight intriguing slant, a grave sweetness about her mouth. The merry frivolous flirt was gone, and a woman stood in her place, one who was self-reliant and capable; kind, gentle and understanding.

Women, Rupe realized, were really tougher-fibered and more durable than men. More adaptable, readier to face and accept the ugliness and cruelty of life and fate. He had observed it in his mother, and he saw it now in Karen. Perhaps it was a compensation for their lack of physical power. Once Rupe would have scoffed at the remotest comparison of his mother to Karen, but a similarity was evident to him now.

In recent fever-ridden dreams, Mom and Jordan, Dodie and Nick and others, now gone, had assumed far more prominence than the living. This had convinced Rupe that he was dying, that he belonged more with those who had departed than with those left alive. In memory he saw his mother more clearly than he saw Karen at his bedside. Rather tall for a woman, straight, slender and young enough to be a sister instead of his mother, quiet and stately with a proudly held head of rich bronze-colored hair and clean blue eyes. Her severely fine features were softened by the sweet sad smile. Killed before fifty by a Kansas winter. Kansas killed everybody. . . .

It was strange to wake up in this high-ceilinged room in Hessler Hall, the stone walls keeping it cool even in midsummer heat. Stranger yet to have Hannibal, former manservant of Clay Hessler, come to shave him and cut his hair. A stolid ebony statue of a man with immense dignity and expert feather-light hands, rumbling at times in a deep solemn bass: "Mistah Clay had his faults, like all us mortals, but he sure was an elegant gentleman. And young Mistah Early the spittin' image of him, so much alike they never was real close. But Miss Karen's the real highborn quality, us folks always figured. A sure-enough young queen, Miss Karen is."

Rupe Maitland was getting better by this time. He could feel it in himself, see it reflected in the faces of Karen and Doc Kinderness, of Melora and Poke Vetter when they came to visit him with news of Frank and the farm. He was still weak and shrunken; a pale, emaciated ghost of himself stared back from the ivory hand mirror Karen held before him, but life and strength were returning slowly. Once more he could taste food, savor a cigarette, take pleasure in the sunrise and sunset colors, interest himself in other people and in outside activities. Birdsong in the trees beyond the tall windows, mourning doves crooning beneath the eaves, the hopeful racket of hammer and saw telling of home building—all these gradually began to form into a living and meaningful pattern to him.

Reef Bassett came to see him, the kinship of men who have fought together in battle between them. "Our big slavers are in Missouri, they say, tryin' to recruit an army to march against Trayborough again. Clay Hessler got away with all his money, Rupe, but he hates to give up this place with all its furnishin's and family belongin's and slaves. Young Early and Asa Sporn are buildin' reputations as gun-fighters, I hear, and Chance Carrick with 'em. Atchinson's tryin' to negotiate with Quantrill, but I doubt if it'll amount to much. Quantrill won't share command with anybody, and the Butcher won't serve as a subordinate."

"I'm goin' after 'em, Reef," said Rupe, "as soon as I can."

"Kind of thought you might," Reef Bassett said. "And you won't have to go alone, Rupe."

Karen came in as Bassett was leaving, graciously accepting his thanks for her services among the wounded and the use of Hessler Hall. She came in and sat down in the chair beside the bed. "You're looking better every day, Rupe, but you're hardly ready for travel. Where's this you're thinking of going?"

"I guess you know, Karen," said Rupe Maitland.

"What good will it do, Rupe? Hasn't there been enough killing?"

"Too much. But there's more to be done yet. I don't see why you've done all this for me, Karen. Knowin' what I've got to do."

She smiled slowly, fondly. "The simplest and oldest reason in the world, Rupert."

Rupe turned his tawny cropped head on the pillow. "No, it'll never work out that way, Karen. I'm goin' after your brother and your father and Asa Sporn."

"That won't solve anything or bring anyone back from the dead."

"Maybe not. But it's got to be done, and I'm goin' to do it."

Karen sighed and shook her lustrous dark head. "Men are like children, little boys that never grow up. Codes of honor like the games the kids play. It doesn't make sense, Rupe."

"It does to me," Rupe Maitland said grimly. "Early murdered Jord. Your father shot Nick Santell in the back. And Asa Sporn killed Dodie Deneen—with a bullet meant for me. There's only one way to pay for things like that, Karen."

"Well, I don't suppose anything can stop you, Rupe."

"Nothin' in the world."

"Whatever you do won't change me," Karen said. "I'll be here, Rupe, waiting for you. No matter what happens."

Rupe shook his blond head, and Karen noticed again how hollow his face was at cheek and temple, the proud nose sharper than ever, the features more angular with cheekbones and jaws jutting bleakly. "It's not for us, Karen. There's too much blood and death between us. It would always be there."

"We'll see, Rupert," she murmured patiently. "There's nothing left between my father and me. I do love Early, in spite of the things he's done. I always will."

"That's natural. But what happened with your father?"

"The way he killed Nick was one thing. Sometime perhaps I'll tell you about the other."

Rupe wondered if it concerned Dodie Deneen. Something had happened to her that night after she left the camp on Mulehead Flats, and he had a vague recollection of a queer exchange of words between Karen and Clay Hessler that afternoon, when Rupe was slumped half-senseless beside Dodie's draped form and Nick Santell's body lay on the floor.

It didn't matter much, anyway. Obviously, he told himself, this relation between Karen and him was a hopeless one. He saw Karen now as a woman to love and respect and marry, but you couldn't very well court a girl when you were bent on hunting down and killing her father and brother. . . .

A month after the battle, Rupe Maitland was up and around, still frail and underweight but gaining rapidly now, walking and exercising a little more each day, and eating with a better appetite. It was wonderful indeed to move about and get outdoors into the fresh air and sunshine, to feel the strength gradually flowing back into muscles and limbs. To have your mind clear, your thoughts free and orderly, your body once more under control.

Chapter 12

Frank Maitland, recovered sufficiently from his wounds for the buggy ride into town, stopped at Hessler Hall while Poke Vetter went on to do the trading and sat with Rupe in the shade of the white-columned veranda overlooking the war-ravaged terraced slope.

"Melora's bearin' up as well as can be expected, Rupe," said Frank, puffing on his pipe. "It's hard for a young widow with the first baby comin', but Mel's got a lot of Millicent in her and she'll weather it through. The Lamberts are still with us and helpin' out a lot, Rupe, along with old Poke. The new barn's up, better than the old one. Sam Sybert and some of the other neighbors were in to help.

"Seems to take trouble and death to bring people close together," Frank went on, "like war and fightin', I guess. And it sure teaches a man that he can't straddle the fence with a fight goin' on all around him."

"You look as good as ever, Dad," said Rupert.

"I'm all right, Rupe, I'm fine. And it won't take long for you to get your weight and strength back now that you're out of bed. You'll be comin' home soon, won't you, Rupe?"

"Well, Dad, I don't know. There's a few things I've got to do."

Frank nodded somberly. "I know, Rupe. You're plannin' on runnin' down the Hesslers. But I wonder if it's worth it now. They're beaten and gone, Rupe, and somebody else'll kill them somewhere, unless they change their ways considerable. Doc tells me Karen kept you alive and pulled you through, Rupe."

"I guess she did, Dad. And that makes it damn hard. But I've got to go after them, just the same. I won't feel right or rest easy until I square it with them."

"I won't try to tell you what to do, Rupe," said his father. "A man knows what he has to do, and if I was younger, I'd feel the same way about it. At my age a man mellows some and forgives easier. So you do what you feel's right and best, Rupe. And when the time comes I might want to go along with you, son."

Rupe smiled warmly at him. "I don't know of a man I'd rather have, Dad," he said sincerely.

"Poke and I missed all the fightin' in here, you know," Frank said. "Old Poke was real put out about it and wouldn't speak a decent word to anybody for days out there on the farm." He chuckled at the memory of Poke's irascibility over missing the fight for Trayborough. "It must have been quite a battle, Rupe."

"It was, Dad," said Rupert. "I wouldn't care to go through another one like it."

"Well, don't start off without lettin' us know, Rupe," said Frank, the pleasant Maitland smile crinkling his newly sunburned cheeks and steady brown eyes. "Poke and I don't want to be left out of everythin'."

They shook hands and Rupe watched his father walk down the long flagstone path to the street as Poke Vetter drove the buggy out from town. Frank limped a little on his left leg, but otherwise showed no effects from the slaver bullets. Waving good-bye to them, Rupe sat down again and watched the rebuilding of the settlement spread out below, where axes were ringing, saws burring and buzzing, hammers pounding and drills grinding. A cheerful busy scene, men whistling and shouting at their work, horses snorting and wheels clattering as teamsters bawled lusty curses and cracked their whips. Pungent with the fine smells of new-cut timber, raw lumber and sawdust, fresh-turned sod and earth, mortar and pitch and oily paint.

Men build and other men tear down, Rupe thought. As soon as the ruins stop smoking and cool off, then building starts again. It was, he thought, the story of life, the history of the world. From ancient Greece to Kansas Territory in this new decade of the 1860s.

A few days later Rupe Maitland was strong enough to try a short ride about the spacious estate on his bay gelding, which had been kept in the stable, well cared for by the Negro hostler. A week after Frank Maitland's visit, Doc Kinderness pronounced Rupe well enough to go home. That evening—his last in Hessler Hall—Rupe sat in his upstairs room, cleaning and oiling his guns. The room, the nicest he'd ever slept in, had been occupied previously by two of the colored maids privileged to live in the big house.

Rupe had come through the battle without losing any of his guns, and someone had salvaged his saber from the front yard for him. With thorough care he worked over Jord's Remington revolver and Dad's Henry rifle and his own Colt six-gun, all the same .44 caliber. The saber, cleaned and polished by Hannibal, Rupe planned to take home and hang up as a souvenir. Sometime it might mean a great deal to his sons, if he ever got around to having any. He had found the woman he wanted to mother his children in Karen Hessler, but only when it was too late to do anything about it. How could a man marry and make love to a girl whose brother and father he had sworn to kill?

Rupe had finished with the guns, and was scrubbing his hands in the washbowl, when Karen rapped lightly and entered at his invitation. She had bathed and changed into a white linen dress after her tour of duty in the hospital, and she looked slim and cool and lovelier than ever, her dark vivid beauty set off by the pure white gown.

"You're leaving, Rupe?" asked Karen, her tilted eyes quizzical and anxious, her black hair burnished in the lamplight.

"Yeah, Doc's kickin' me out in the mornin', Karen."

She glanced at the rifle and the shell belt with its holstered guns. "The tools of your trade are ready, I see," Karen remarked with a faintly twisted smile.

Rupe's eyes were sober. "You've got to admit they're kind of necessary tools in this country, and at this time."

"Yes, yes, I know," she said wearily. "Are you going home—first?"

"For a while." He finished drying his hands and draped the towel on the rack.

"Your father's a fine man, Rupe, and your sister's a sweet girl. They've suffered enough already, it seems to me. Why don't you stay with them, Rupert?"

"I will—until the time comes to go. And then I'll be back."

"You can't tell. Your luck can't last forever."

Rupe Maitland shrugged his broad sloped shoulders.

Karen moved closer, her fragrance flooding his sense and firing his blood. "Rupe, we've lost enough in this business, both of us. Do we have to lose one another, too?"

"I'm afraid so, Karen. It's somethin' outside of us, that we can't control."

"We *could* control it; but you won't listen to reason," Karen Hessler said. "You left me once before, Rupe, and that was my fault for being such a silly flighty fool. This time—if you go—it's your own fault, Rupert. And there won't be any coming back."

"I've got to go," Rupe said simply, fighting down the desire to sweep her into his arms.

"I love you, Rupe," said Karen, "I always have, although I didn't know enough to realize it once. I liked Jord a lot, too, but that was different. You've always been the one, and you always will be."

"You're the one for me, too, Karen. But it just wasn't meant for us to be together."

"Can't you let them go, Rupe, forget about them?"

"I've got to live with myself," Rupe said. "I can't do it without settlin' with them."

"All right, Rupe," she said, swaying against him, her face on his shoulder. "Nothing can change you. But my love won't change, either."

He held her lightly, comfortingly. "Yes, it will, Karen—after that. There won't be anythin' left."

She moved her head from side to side against his chest. "Time will answer that for sure, but I know already. You don't understand women in love, Rupert. The way I'm in love."

"What I've got to do can't leave room for love," Rupe

said, his tone edged with the same bitterness that showed in his gray eyes and in the set of his lean haggard face. "There'll be hate instead, Karen. It can't be any different." He felt hollow and hopeless, knowing his words were true, and would sentence him to live out his life—if he lived—in loneliness and sterile waste.

"Promise me one thing, Rupe," she pleaded, tipping back her dark head and staring up at him. "That you'll come back and tell me about it. Give me a chance to decide for myself."

"Yes, I'll do that, Karen. But it won't do any good."

Her arms slid about his limber waist, locking tight as she lifted her lips for him, and Rupe crushed her close and lowered his mouth onto the fullness of hers, the pure flame of it leaping through them, blending them into one, lifting them in rapture. Then, with tremendous effort Rupe pulled himself out of that shimmering flight and back to stark reality, holding the girl at arm's length. "You'd better go, Karen."

"If you want me to, Rupe," she whispered. "But you know—you *must* know—that I'm yours, Rupe. Always and forever, I belong to you."

"You know it's useless!" he said, his voice hoarse and harsh with barely suppressed emotion.

"Well, come to me, Rupe. When you get back—when it's all over. You'll come to me then, won't you, Rupert?"

Rupe Maitland tried to keep the anguish from his words. "Yes. I'll come to you then, Karen."

Two weeks after his discharge from the hospital at Hessler Hall, Rupert Maitland was working on the farm when Poke Vetter rode up with the letter from Reef Bassett in Missouri. The men they wanted were in St. Louis. The Hesslers, Asa Sporn and Chance Carrick. Atchinson had gone south, and the others were thinking of following him down the Mississippi before long. Rupe had better start at once if he wanted to catch them before they left. Reef would try to meet him at the Riverview House in St. Louis by the end of the next week.

"Poke and I are goin' along with you, Rupe," said

Frank Maitland. "There's four of them, and there'll be four of us with Reef Bassett. I'd kind of like to see St. Louis and the Mississippi again, anyway."

"You're damn tootin', Frank," said Poke Vetter, his one eye twinkling. "We missed all the fun in Trayborough, so we sure ain't goin' to git dealt out of this jamboree."

"I'll tend to the farm all right, Frank," said True Lambert. "And the missus'll take care of Mellie."

"Thanks, True, I was countin' on you folks," Frank told him gratefully. "Sam and the neighbors'll help out with the last hayin' and we'll be back in time for the reapin' and harvestin'."

They checked horses and saddle gear, packed saddlebags and bedrolls, guns and ammunition. Sam Sybert rattled into the yard in his buckboard with the news that war between the North and South had really begun, with fighting in West Virginia and Carthage, Missouri. But as yet Rupe Maitland wasn't interested in the war. The raid on Harpers Ferry was history and Old John Brown had been hanged at Charlestown. Southern states had seceded from the Union; Fort Sumter had been fired on last April, and President Lincoln had called for volunteers. . . . And all Rupe could think of was bringing the Hesslers to bay.

They made their brief farewells and started out, two middle-aged men and young Rupe Maitland, his gray eyes old beyond his years and his broad mouth stern and bitter.

Melora Maitland Santell watched the last two men of her family ride away with Poke Vetter, her blue eyes washed with tears, her golden head high and proud, the new life stirring even stronger within her. She hoped her baby would be a boy with red hair, and grow up a man like his father Nick, and her own father Frank, and her brothers Jord and Rupert.

The three riders struck across country in an easterly direction toward the Missouri border, their route in general to follow the Kansas River to its conjunction with the Missouri, and then follow the Big Muddy, except for its northward bends, on to St. Louis. They passed lonely homesteads, isolated ranches, and tiny settlements in the wilderness, driving on at a good gait.

It was over three hundred miles to St. Louis, the entire breadth of Missouri to be traversed, and the blazing heat of early August beat down upon them with pitiless intensity, wilting and sapping the energy of horses and riders alike. Poke Vetter knew the country and had friends along the way. Rupe wondered how one man could live long enough to know all the territory and people that Poke did. Under his guidance they took time-saving cutoffs, hit the easiest river crossings, and exchanged mounts here and there, in order to maintain the steady killing pace.

Usually alert and aware of his surroundings, Rupe Maitland remembered little of that long grueling trek eastward, riding so withdrawn and silent the older men worried about him, impatient to attain his objective. Still slightly underweight, drawn a little fine, Rupe felt and looked almost as fit and strong as ever, his lean features polished to a bronze tone again by the sun and wind. But there were dark crescents under his clear gray eyes, and new lines cut in deep arcs about the wide mouth, and in additional creases on the rare occasions he smiled.

By day Rupe rode with his father and Poke, but in his dreams at night he was riding with Jordan and Nick Santell. It was amazing how often he dreamt of them, and particularly of Jord. The world was an empty place with Jord gone, and while time might ease the sorrow, nothing could ever take Jord's place. Whenever Rupe saw or heard something that pleased or amused him, his first impulse was to tell Jord about it, for they had always shared beauty and humor and pathos in this manner. Awake and asleep now, Rupe had visions of Jord smiling that incomparable smile of his, or laughing with his bright brown head tossed back. Nobody smiled and laughed like Jordan. And Rupe thought of their boyhood fights, wincing at the memory of his fists striking that fine beloved face. Rupe always won, having the psychological advantage of the elder brother, and Jord always promised to get even someday.

At Independence, they heard that wholesale fighting had broken out in the East with engagements at Big Bethel and Laurel Hill, West Virginia, and the War Between the States was on in earnest. In Jefferson City, this was confirmed with details about a great battle in Virginia on July 21, 1861, a Confederate victory, which the Southerners called Manassas and the Union called Bull Run.

Jefferson was in a tumult of excitement over the war and an impending battle near Springfield, Missouri, where General Nathaniel Lyon with a Union force of six thousand was moving against a Confederate army of twelve thousand under General Ben McCulloch, encamped at Wilson's Creek. War on such a mammoth scale made the Trayborough affair seem like a very minor skirmish indeed, but it failed to deter the Maitlands and Vetter from their private mission of revenge.

Union recruiting officers tried to press them into service, eyeing big rangy young Rupert with special interest. He told them: "We've got a job of our own to do first. I'll probably be joinin' up when that's done."

"We been fightin' this war for years out in Kansas," Poke Vetter told them sourly. "Nobody has to beg to get us into battle."

They rode on along the broad Missouri River, sweeping eastward between high wooded bluffs, with stern-wheel steamers wallowing heavy-laden in the yellow-brown water, their mournful whistles echoing over plain and forest.

"Be a helluva note if our slavers have gone and joined up with McCulloch's Rebs," grumbled Poke Vetter.

"I wouldn't be surprised if Reef Bassett was with the Union army," Frank said. "But he wouldn't go without leavin' some message for us at the Riverview House."

"McCulloch's Texans might draw Chance Carrick and Asa Sporn," mused Rupe.

"I'd like to serve under Nat Lyon myself," Poke said. "He done a good job keepin' the St. Louis arsenal from the Confederates."

One late afternoon, with the last lap of the journey ahead of them, they rode wearily into a small river-port town, and paused to watch the *Frontier Maid* swing up to the dock. Poke Vetter suggested that they board it to rest themselves for the showdown before them. Paying the purser their passage fare to St. Louis, they left their horses among others on the lower deck and climbed aloft to the hurricane deck for a few rounds of drinks in the lavishly ornamented saloon. After plodding miles in the saddle, there was a sense of luxurious comfort and well-being here, but Rupe soon left them to go on deck with a tall drink in his hand.

The last time Rupe had traveled by water was when the family came West twelve years ago, and he was fifteen, Jord thirteen, and Melora eleven. Leaning on the rail watching the enormous dripping paddle wheels revolve, he recalled wistfully the boyish excitement he had shared with Jord at the time. The captain of one boat, taking a liking to the boys, had brought them up to the glassed-in pilothouse, and even let them hold the great wheel for a moment. Then Jord had got into an argument with a hulking oversized boy, and big brother Rupe had stepped in and thrashed the bully. He could see exactly the way Jord looked, brown eyes afire and bright curls tousled, saying in almost tearful anger, "I could've licked him myself, Rupe! You're always buttin' in on me. Why don't you mind your own business?"

Feeling melancholy, Rupe went back to the saloon for another drink with Dad and Poke. They had learned that McCulloch's Confederates had won a bloody battle at Wilson's Creek on August tenth, with both sides losing over a thousand men. And twice-wounded Nathaniel Lyon, his horse shot under him, had been killed as he swung into another saddle to lead a final charge for the nearly defeated Northern troops.

"We're goin' to miss that boy," Poke Vetter said, his one eye grave as he shook his grizzled head. "He was a real soldier and fightin' man, that Nat Lyon."

Rupert was mildly angered to hear of another Southern victory; it seemed they were winning them all. But the war was still remote, almost irrelevant to him, and would be until he had finished his personal war with the Hesslers. The dreadful casualties seemed unreal also. Having seen so much death at close hand, the deaths of those nearest to him like Jord and Nick and Dodie Deneen, Rupe had been drained of sympathy for outside losses like those at Wilson's Creek.

He had suffered and lost too much himself to be deeply moved by the pain and bereavement of strangers. Still numb and shocked from his own grief, Rupe couldn't feel for the rest of humanity as he had in the past. Somehow, he'd become hardened and calloused. This apparent heartlessness dismayed him, but he could not help it. A man can only bleed so much, and he was bled dry.

Rupe surmised that he might have to keep a close watch on his father and Poke Vetter, once they had reached St. Louis. Knowing how it was with Karen and Rupe, they probably figured on taking care of the Hesslers themselves, to spare Rupe the task of killing the father and brother of the girl he loved. But Rupe wanted Clay and Early himself, even if it meant losing Karen and wrecking his whole future. It looked as if that future would be dedicated to endless warfare anyway, with no place in it for love and marriage and raising children. And he had his duty to Jord and Nick and Dodie, to all the others who had died because of the Hesslers and their kind. He could still hear Nick Santell's dying voice: *"Get him, Rupe! Get the slavin' snake for me."*

On deck again with darkness on land and water and a saber-like golden moon hanging slender in the star-sown heavens, Rupe heard the chant of Negroes from the boiler-room depths, and it started again the weird chanting in his head. A primitive dirge that had been running through his mind at night when he stared at the moon, ever since that terrible afternoon in the square at Trayborough. He had no idea where it came from, but it had been with him at Hessler's Pond, on Mulehead Flats, in his bed in Hessler Hall, and on the trail across Missouri. For the first time he consciously put words to it: *"Moon, moon, way up high/ Why you let my brother die?"* Just that, over and over again. It had come out of nowhere, and went on forever when he saw the moon.

The nighttime glare of St. Louis awed Rupe Maitland at first, the monstrous size and dinning noise of the sprawled city seemed to dwarf him to pinpoint obscurity and insignificance, overwhelming him completely. The docks were lined with enormous and palatial side-wheelers, loading and unloading or lying idle, with lesser craft clustered about them. The levee was a brawling riot of activity in the garish flicker of oil lamps and lanterns, pitch- and tar-barrel flares. Freight wagons jammed the cobble-stone street, pedestrians swarmed the walks and wharves, and huge warehouses loomed over the seething waterfront. Stevedores labored, stripped to the waist and sweat-shining, amidst towering stacks of baled, crated and barreled merchandise, with windlasses creaking and cables groaning overhead in the darkness.

The *Frontier Maid* nosed ponderously into the land-ing, alongside a bigger vessel bearing the name *Mississippi Belle*, agleam with fresh paint and polished brass. "For New Orleans," Poke Vetter said. "If our men are still here, it's likely they're booked on her." Ropes snaked out from the *Maid* and were snubbed fast to pilings, while deck-hands stood by to lower the gangplanks. From somewhere across the light-splashed oily shimmer of black water came the scream of whistles in deep-toned mourning and bells clanged their lively jangle through the general bedlam.

Rupe Maitland felt lost in a foreign world as they led their mounts down a sagging cleated plank to the turmoil of the pier and the cobbled street. Poke Vetter handed his reins to Rupe and said he'd be right back after making inquiries aboard the *Belle*. Frank Maitland, reins wrapped about his wrist, filled and lighted his pipe with satisfaction, and Rupe marveled at his father's calmness in this strange turbulent melee. Everybody acted drunk or crazy, and there was a mad carnival atmosphere about the entire scene.

Poke returned nodding and grinning wickedly, looking like a pirate in soiled buckskins with that black patch over his eyeless socket. "They're on the passenger list and she's sailin' in the mornin', men. Come on, let's go find Reef and git organized for business."

Poke Vetter, as much at home here as in the wilderness, stepped into his saddle and led the way, Frank and Rupe mounting and following him through the thronged confusion of vehicles and people. Dockside saloons, their open doors spilling out yellow gaslight and roaring animal sounds into the riptide traffic of Front Street, at first made Rupe uneasy, but soon he became acclimated and caught some of the lusty spirit of the booming port. It was a relief to find themselves just in time to get the men they were after. A few more hours and they'd have been too late.

At the Riverview House, they left their horses at the livery barn in the rear, with instructions as to their care and feeding. Carrying saddlebags and rifles, they walked around front to the lobby, Rupe scanning the crowded thoroughfare and wondering aloud if the Hesslers would be staying in this hotel. "Naw, they wouldn't put up in a waterfront dive like this," Poke said. "They'll be in some flossy joint uptown, or stayin' with some of their fancy Southern friends."

They signed the book for rooms and found that Reef Bassett was registered in number 43, which meant that everything was working out fine. Rupe was about to question the clerk when Poke elbowed him into silence. Their rooms, like Reef's, were on the third or top floor. There was no response when they knocked at Bassett's door, so they left their gear locked in their rooms and went out to a nearby barbershop for shaves, haircuts and baths. Back at the Riverview, finding Reef Bassett still absent, they changed into fresh clothing and moved on to a restaurant recommended by Poke, where they had an excellent late supper.

Feeling clean and refreshed, Rupe relaxed in the quiet pleasant atmosphere of the cafe, talking and laughing more than he had in days, enjoying the drinks and the food to the utmost. The surprising worldliness of his father and Poke gave him confidence, and Rupe was beginning to feel comfortably at ease in these new environs. Lighting cigars with their brandy, they lounged in leisurely satisfaction, and Rupe felt quite like a man of the world himself.

"There's somethin' to be said for civilization after all," Frank remarked, gratified as much by Rupe's pleasure as his own.

"I can stand it, Frank, in small doses," said Poke Vetter. "But I'd sure hate to live in it all the time."

Afterward they strolled about the hectic crowded streets to digest their meals and look the town over, keeping a lookout for the Hessler party and listening to snatches of war talk on all sides. Men from all walks of life formed constant bizarre processions in the lamplight. Frock-coated silk-hatted dignitaries and politicians, with well-tailored business and professional men. Soldiers in blue uniforms, frontiersmen in buckskin, farmers in overalls or their Sunday best. Sleek cold-eyed Mississippi gamblers, and lean, wiry riders with sagging gun belts and spurred boots. Lumbermen in plaid shirts and stagged pants, river boatmen in rakish caps and striped jerseys. Bearded trappers in smoke-stained buckskin, and prospectors, pale-faced clerks and sunburned emigrants, stolid blanket Indians and furtive-eyed Negroes.

Uptown they made the rounds of the hotels, but failed to find the men they wanted registered at any of them. A search of most of the saloons and several gambling halls disclosed no sign of the Hesslers, Carrick and Sporn, nor were they anywhere to be seen in the massed streets and squares of the city. "I got a notion they're celebratin' this last night in some fancy high-priced honky-tonk," Poke Vetter said, spitting a stream of tobacco juice into the gutter.

Some of the establishments they visited were so grand and glittering that Rupe was hesitant about entering them, but his father and Poke seemed as much at ease in these elaborate layouts as they were in Gunnarsson's old stone barroom back in Trayborough. After adjusting himself, Rupe lost his nervousness and came to realize that the most pretentious places weren't so very different from the sawdust saloons on the frontier. There was as much drunkenness and as many rough elements, for all the dazzling chandeliers, gleaming gilt-framed mirrors, gaudy brass and crystals, the oil paintings and the bold-eyed women in low-cut silk and satin gowns. The perfumed atmosphere was heady and exhilarating, Rupe found, but at the same time faintly revolting. It wasn't an unalloyed delight to him to see so many pretty young women parading their charms in such a flagrant style.

After a fruitless tour of the dance halls that might have lured Early Hessler and Asa Sporn, they drifted back toward the waterfront to look again for Reef Bassett.

In the Riverview House, they rapped once more at Number 43 and again there was no answer, the room unlighted and the door locked. They were about to turn away when Poke Vetter crouched suddenly and ran his forefinger along the doorsill. His finger came away flaked and darkly stained. Poke straightened, his one eye fixed grimly on Rupert, the lines in his seamed leathery face deeper than ever.

"Break it in, Rupe. I reckon Reef's been here right along."

Grasping the knob, Rupe slammed a shoulder into the door and heaved with all the power from his ankles up. It gave with a rending crash, opening inward until it jammed against something on the floor. In the slant of light from the wall-bracketed lamp in the corridor, they saw the boots and legs of a man who lay stretched facedown on the carpet. Flicking a match aflame, Rupe moved inside and lighted the lamp on the table, while Frank closed the door behind them. It was the broad massive bulk of Reef Bassett, dead for hours, the back of his shirt slashed in three places and encrusted with blood. There were three deep stab wounds in his wide back, any one of which would have been fatal.

"Murder again," Rupe Maitland said softly. "With the Hesslers, it's always murder."

Chapter 13

Alone in bed in his single room in the Riverview House on the waterfront of St. Louis, Rupert Maitland could not sleep that night. He missed his mother, feeling like a little boy away from home for the first time, scared and lonely in a strange bedroom. Mother was a comfort when everything else failed. She made you feel good, even with things going wrong all around you. The one person who'd forgive you, no matter what you did. She was dead and buried on a cedar hummock behind the log farmhouse in Kansas.

And Jordan in his grave beside her. Rupe was lonesome for Jord, more than ever. Things were fun with Jord, everything was fun. He wanted to see Jord's face light up, see him smile and hear him laugh. There was nobody like Jord, there never would be. And he was dead at twenty-five. *"Moon, moon, way up high, why, why, why?"*

Rupe missed Nick Santell's thin tough face and reckless blue eyes, his cocky auburn head and jeering cursing voice. And Dodie Deneen with her red-gold hair and jade-green eyes and the full-blown body that had taken the slug Asa Sporn threw at Rupe, giving her life to save his.

He thought of big, friendly Joe Gayle and lean, quick Eastlach and chubby, moon-faced Lem Sybert. Dead, all dead. Trim, precise Henry Holdcroft in a bed of Cherokee roses, and solid, rock-jawed Reef Bassett in a cheap dingy hotel room down the hall. Rupe wondered who had driven that blade into Reef's back. Chance Carrick was handy with a knife, they said; it was probably the tall buzzard-faced Texan.

Spread the guilt around, Rupe Maitland thought somberly. Early Hessler had started it with the murder of Jord. Asa Sporn had killed Dodie, and Clay Hessler had shot Nick in the back. Now Carrick had knifed Reef Bassett, and Atchinson had hundreds of lives to answer for.

They'd been lucky so far. Early had escaped from the cabin on the shore of Hessler's Pond, the same night Shaw Tattam, Preacher Pratt and two more slavers died. And they all got away from Hessler Hall when the Yankees retook Trayborough, except for Huber Northrup and Elwood Kivett, who went down in that cavalry charge. *But they wouldn't get away this time, by God!*

Rupe Maitland got quietly out of bed and started dressing in the dark. He understood that passengers weren't allowed on board the night before sailing, but the Hesslers had enough money to cut through a lot of regulations and customs. Rupe had a sudden strong hunch that they were already on the *Mississippi Belle*, hiding out there after the stabbing of Bassett. He debated whether or not to awaken Dad and Poke, finally deciding against it. He didn't want them hurt any more. They were good men to have along, but Rupe wouldn't risk their lives. This was his job and he'd do it alone. Dad and Poke were a little old for this kind of work, a bit slow for gunmen like the Hesslers and Sporn and Carrick.

He put on a dark blue shirt instead of the white one he'd worn earlier, and knotted a loose scarf in place of the string tie. Strapping on his gun belt, he tied the holster-ends to his thighs, Jord's Remington on the left leg, his own Colt on the right. Then Rupe pulled on his dark suit coat and the black hat with its flat crown and wide brim. He was ready to go now, ready for anything. Carefully unlocking and opening the door, he slipped silently into the corridor. The double room Dad and Poke had across the way was dark and still. Treading on tiptoe, feeling ridiculously like a truant schoolboy, Rupe moved toward the stairway. Once a sound, seemingly from their room, stopped him. Rupe decided it was just the creaking of old timbers and went on and down the two flights of stairs.

The barroom off the lobby was still lighted and open

for business, and Rupe shouldered through the batwing doors. There weren't many customers at this late hour, perhaps a dozen scattered along the bar. Rupe ordered whiskey and built himself a cigarette. The man on his left, leaning on spread elbows, wore a greasy visored cap and turtleneck sweater and had the appearance of a river boatman. He turned bleary unfocused eyes and surveyed Rupe's rangy figure from the wide-brimmed hat to the riding boots, lingering on the low-slung guns.

"Two-gun man," he mumbled. "Brother, let's you and me clean house here."

Rupe smiled and shook his head. "I'm a peace-lovin' pilgrim."

"What you packin' them guns for, then?"

"Self-defense."

"Ain't you big enough, friend, not to need them irons?"

"Where I come from they count more than size," Rupe drawled, tossing off his drink and turning away.

The man caught his arm. "Don't hurry, cowboy. Buy you a drink. Last night in town, lonesome, my gal run out, left me flat. Hell with her, huh? Plenty more and better-lookers down in New Orleans. Bartender, pour two here and leave the bottle."

Annoyed at first, Rupe was interested now by the reference to New Orleans. Settling back on the bar, he said, "You're shippin' out?"

"That's right, mate. Come mornin'."

"*Mississippi Belle?*" hazarded Rupert.

"Right again—best boat on the river. Them others are all mudscows alongside the *Belle*."

"Any passengers aboard now?"

"Not till mornin', mister."

Rupe studied his glass. "I'd sure like to get on board a big steamer like that."

"Why not?" laughed his companion. "I'll take you on. Against the rules, but it don't matter. All drunk tonight, captain and crew. You wanta see her, I'll show you, cowboy."

"Tonight?"

"Sure, right now. Cost you nothin' but a coupla pints. One for me, one for the watch."

"Cheap enough, sailor." Rupe bought two pint bottles of whiskey, handing one to his guide and pocketing the other. "Let's go."

"We're off, mate." Hooking his arm through Rupe's, he led him weaving toward the swing doors. "Someday you can gimme a ride on your horse, huh?" He laughed in uproarious delight.

Front Street was submerged in a dense damp fog, the streetlamps shrouded pale and eerie, and a light, misty rain sifted down in the night. "My name's Mulherrin and they call me Mully or Mullet or The Herrin'," confided the other, and broke into bawdy rollicking song as they tramped toward the docks, the cobblestones slick and glistening underfoot, the rain drizzling through the gray vapors that rolled in from the river.

My luck's in, thought Rupe Maitland. *The cards are coming my way. I feel sure the Hessler bunch is on board. This hunch'll have to work out better than my other one did that night at the headwaters of the Cygne when Joe Gayle and Eastlach died.* That seemed a long time ago now. A lot of other men, both good and bad, had gone under since then. Rupe had a fleeting mental image of Karen Hessler and willed it coldly out of his mind. This was no time to be thinking of her, nor of anyone or anything except the job at hand.

"How about shootin' off them guns, friend?" inquired Mulherrin.

"They're empty, Mully."

"Plenty bullets in your belt, cowboy."

"We don't want to get arrested, Mully," said Rupe. "Sing us another song."

Mulherrin obliged with a bawdy ditty as they neared the wharves, but Rupe was listening to the whisper of rain on stone, water lapping around the piles and washing against the levee, the groaning of timbers and sighing of hawsers, a foghorn's blast from the stream. The mist swirled in, thinning and thickening, and the boats loomed ghostly in the grayness, faintly streaked here and there by frosty yellow glimmers of light.

Hearing footsteps behind them, or fancying he did, Rupe Maitland glanced back occasionally but could see nothing in the shifting fog, the smell and taste of which reminded him of that early morning on Mulehead Flats, moving to the attack on Trayborough. Drunk as Mulherrin was, he led the way unerringly to the gangplank of the *Mississippi Belle*. The man on watch was half-asleep, but he woke up quickly when Rupe handed him the flat bottle and asked, "Where are the passengers?"

The watchman caressed the bottle and frowned at Rupe. "You a friend of theirs? Sleepin' in their staterooms, most likely. What's goin' on here anyway, Mullet?"

"Drink your booze and shut your gab, Piper," said Mulherrin. "My good friend here wants to see the best packet on the river, that's all. A pint oughta pay for that, hadn't it, Piper? Come on, cowboy, I'll show you around."

"Quiet, Mully," cautioned Rupe. "I've got friends aboard and I want to surprise them, see?"

"How the hell'd they get on?" Mulherrin muttered. "Never mind, we'll surprise 'em."

The lower deck was piled with boxes and bales, crates and barrels. They climbed to the next one above and looked about in the clammy fog, but no lights showed from any of the stateroom portholes or the saloon. There were dim sounds of movement at the bow, and they paced quietly in that direction. Listening intently, Rupe thought he could hear footsteps and voices from above, and the clump of boots from the midship area behind them. The rain filtered down, thin and muffled in the mist, and he couldn't be certain of anything in this gray drenched world.

Rupe Maitland wished now he had brought Dad and Poke Vetter along. One against four was cutting it pretty thin. He'd get one or two of them, but he couldn't count on any more than that, unless he was awful lucky. He'd get the Hesslers anyway. Shot through the heart, he'd live long enough to kill Early and Clay. And if it broke right he might drop Asa Sporn, too, if he got enough of a jump on them. Rupe was sure to die himself, barring miracles, but better

·him than Dad and Poke. When men got to be that age, they shouldn't have to go out and fight. Anyhow, most of the best people he knew were dead.

"Wait here, Mully," whispered Rupe. "They're up on the Texas deck, I guess, likely in the pilothouse. I'm goin' up and surprise hell out of 'em."

Mulherrin was puzzled but too far gone in drink to bother his muddled head about it. Walking unsteadily toward the starboard side, he uncorked his pint, drank deeply, and hung happily over the rail, staring raptly at the sunken misted glow of St. Louis in the fog and rain.

Climbing the wet, gritty iron ladder to the hurricane deck, Rupe heard somebody moving forward above him, but he paid little attention, positive now that the pilot's castle was occupied, thankful for the vapors that cloaked him and everything else, the rain that obscured the sound of his movements. They were on the port side of the glassed-in wheelhouse, and from the ladder top Rupe crawled to the starboard rail. Low, slurred voices reached him, unmistakably Southern in accent, and Rupe Maitland went cold and rigid as he crouched there, spine chilled and prickling, scalp creeping tight, throat aching-dry and heart pumping hard enough to make breathing difficult.

Rising slightly as the mist momentarily lifted, Rupe could see their blurred, shadowy figures through the rain-streaked glass. Three of them—only three instead of four. Squinting and straining his eyes in the gloom, Rupe gradually made out the towering beak-faced Chance Carrick, elegant, graceful Clay Hessler, and the slim whip-thong form of Asa Sporn. But Early Hessler was missing, he realized with a sinking sensation. Early wasn't here, unless that was he, coming forward on the deck below, already mounting the ladder by this time. Someone was on the ladder at any rate, but Rupe wasn't letting that stop him at this stage of the game.

From the rail, Rupe crouched into the shadow of the pilothouse and drew his .44 Colt. Bent low, he edged across the broad front of the glassed enclosure, left shoulder pressed to the wall, right hand gripping the gun. Against these odds he had to take every available advantage. . . .

"What's that?" Asa Sporn's voice demanded sharply, and through misted glass Rupe caught the swift blurred motion as Sporn whipped for his gun and stalked toward the forward corner of the wheelhouse. Rupe Maitland lined his Colt, thumbing the hammer as Sporn cleared the glass cornice and walked directly into the blaring orange muzzle-blast from Rupe's gun.

The slug lifted and twirled Asa Sporn's slender body against the pilothouse, his right shoulder smashing the thick glass into a splintered jangling cascade. Sporn fired once, and Rupe felt the scorching breath of it as he leveled off from the recoil and let go again, the gun flaring bright and loud in the fog, bucking hard against Rupe's hand and wrist. Asa Sporn coughed blood and crumpled writhing on the corner, clawed at the jagged broken glass, twisting and falling away in a disjointed stagger, pitching headlong into a slack motionless sprawl on the fore bridge.

Thinking only of getting the other two, Rupe Maitland lunged recklessly forward and rounded the corner of the wheelhouse. The Southerners were charging at him, instead of breaking away aft, and they collided with a jarring crash in the mist-wreathed darkness, entangled too close for gunplay, lashing out with gun barrels and fists, elbows and knees, in a mad, reeling welter. Driving with long legs and wrenching shoulders, Rupe split them apart and tried to clear his gun hand as they closed back in and grappled at him.

Whirling and bursting away with explosive fury, Rupe Maitland slashed his gun barrel across Clay Hessler's aristocratic forehead, beating him all the way back against the port rail, where he hung stunned and sagging, the blood pouring into his eyes and down the proud, insolent face. Pivoting cleanly, Rupe was ripping his left fist into Carrick's vulture-face, just as Chance's Colt barrel clipped viciously down on Rupe's flat-crowned hat and skull. The blows landed simultaneously. Dazed, his knees buckling, Rupe still followed through savagely with that punch, snapping the high evil head and knocking Carrick into a long backward lurch that left him spread-eagled against the pilothouse.

But Rupe Maitland himself was sinking slowly to his knees, jolted clear to the base of his spine, his head roaring and splitting, his sense fading, his gun hand flat and numb on the deck. Fog poured in and blotted out everything for a hushed interval, and Rupe thought he had lost consciousness until the air cleared again. He was still kneeling there, unable to lift his gun, with Clay Hessler draped loosely on the railing and Chance Carrick still slumped lankily against the glass wall. All three of them half-senseless, impotent and helpless, as another rush of mist enveloped the enclosure in dense dripping white clouds.

Rocking sick and weak on his knees, Rupe Maitland fought to retain his senses and raise his gun, expecting at any instant the blinding flashes and the hot tear of lead through his body. Then his father's clear voice rang out through the coiling vapor, like something in an impossible dream: "This way, Clay. I'm takin' you!" Looking up with agonized eyes, Rupe saw Frank Maitland standing there aft of the wheelhouse, broad and solid, and with the Henry rifle leveled at his waistline.

Clay Hessler's head and gun arm jerked up spasmodically and fire spurted roaring from his hand, angled high and wild, lost in the deep whiplike crash of the Henry, the flame spearing Clay's shuddering body against the rail. Another blast from the carbine held firmly at Frank's hip and lancing fire through the haze, and Clay Hessler, arms upflung and pistol exploding aimlessly into the fogged sky, toppled back over the rail and dropped out of sight. The splash rose faintly through the shot-echoing night as he struck the water.

Then Poke Vetter's voice came from his stand beside Frank: "Over here, Chance! You're mine, I reckon."

Chance Carrick heaved and whirled off the glass wall, his gun blazing in the grayness. Poke Vetter, slouched, languid, almost negligent, threw down his long-barreled revolver with careless ease and hammered home one shot. Grunting and gagging, the tall Texan folded slowly and stiffened out at last at the foot of the pilothouse. Rupe could let go then and he did, leaning sidewise abruptly, the wet deck rising swiftly against him, the impact never reaching him through the quick blackening-out of everything, as the reverberating gunfire died away over the mist-laden Mississippi . . .

When Rupe came to, his head in his father's lap and Poke standing over them, his first words were: "Where's Early Hessler?"

"Chance said he went to join McCulloch's Confederates," said Frank. "Chance lived for a few minutes. You goin' to be all right, Rupe? We thought you were shot, at first."

"Just a headache," Rupe said. "That sonofabitch Early!"

Poke Vetter grinned and spat. "We can't have everythin', Rupe. Three of 'em ain't a bad night's work."

Rupe Maitland sat up, shook his head experimentally, and clambered slowly to his feet. "I sure messed it up," he said disgustedly.

"You young fellahs are always tryin' to hog the fun," Poke complained, his one eye atwinkle. "But you didn't do bad. You kinda softened 'em and set 'em up for us, Rupe."

Rupe smiled ruefully. "I forgot old men don't sleep at night. And a damn good thing for me they don't!"

"Hell, you would've got 'em all yourself, kid," Poke said gruffly. "But your pa and me kinda wanted to horn in on this one, seein' as we rode all the way out here for this shindig."

Mulherrin stumbled out of the fog, staring at the two dead men and handing the bottle to Rupe. "Maybe you need one now, cowboy. It looks like you surprised your friends, all right. You do pretty fair with them empty guns, friend. I'd hate to see you go when you got bullets in 'em!"

Rupe Maitland laughed and took a swig, but the feeling of dissatisfaction and failure persisted. Early Hessler had got away again. The world was well rid of Clay Hessler and Asa Sporn and Chance Carrick, but Early was still alive and walking the earth. It wasn't any good without Early. It wouldn't be settled and right until Early Hessler was dead, too.

"Let's get out of here before the law comes," Poke Vetter suggested.

Rupe Maitland touched his gashed throbbing head and
looked at the blood on his fingers. "You knew they were on
this boat," he accused. "You were comin' after them without
me, Dad."

"No, Rupe," said Frank Maitland, with his grave
smile. "We were just guessin'—same as you."

They left the awed Mulherrin and the *Mississippi
Belle*, holding off the watch and other aroused crewmen at
gunpoint, and walked back to the hotel in the misty rain.
Frank and Poke felt a quiet satisfaction, but Rupe was
disconsolate and depressed. All this way, all that fighting,
and Early Hessler still lived.

"Maybe it's just as well, Rupe, that Early wasn't there
and you didn't get to kill Clay," said his father. "This way, it
won't be there between you and Karen."

"It'll be there," Rupe said. "I'm still goin' to get Early."

"Not much chance, Rupe, if he's in the army."

"His time'll come, Dad. I suppose I might as well
enlist, myself."

"Come home first, anyway," advised Frank. "There'll
be time enough to get into it, Rupe. This is goin' to be a
long war."

Poke Vetter squirted tobacco juice at a lamp post.
"There's always a chance that Early'll drift back to Hessler
Hall. Better come home with us and see before you light off
anywhere else, Rupe."

Rupe Maitland nodded. "Yes, I'll do that, I guess."

"And we'd better move out tonight, boys," Frank said.
"The Riverview's a mite too close for comfort, with all the
law they've got in St. Louis."

Chapter 14

They got out of St. Louis that night in the fog and rain, and slept in a crumbling abandoned shanty north of the city, toward the valley of the Missouri. They had made arrangements for Reef Bassett's body to be shipped home to his ranch outside of Trayborough, and that was all they could do for the major. Early morning saw them in the saddle again, heading westward with the rising sun at their backs, the weather clear and bright with the promise of sweltering heat as the day progressed.

The return trip was long and wearisome, with Rupert even more aloof, more brooding and bitter than on the ride east. For him the journey was almost wasted, the mission a failure, even though Clay Hessler and Asa Sporn and Chance Carrick had died. Rupe Maitland was still sick, and only the death of Early Hessler would make him well.

By exchanging mounts at the same places, they returned horses to their owners along the route. In Jefferson City, Rupe broke the jaw of a Union recruiting sergeant who taunted him about not being in uniform. At Independence, Frank and Poke had to haul Rupe off a saloon bruiser who picked a fight and got himself beaten insensible for it. In an ugly murderous mood, Rupe might have killed the man with his bare hands if his father and Vetter hadn't dragged him away.

According to rumor, McCulloch's Rebel army was marching on Fort Scott, Missouri, and Rupert wanted to turn off in that direction at once, until Frank and Poke impressed on him the utter hopelessness of trying to find one Confederate in the military maneuvering of massed thousands.

"You've got to learn to be patient, Rupe," said Frank Maitland, worried about the embittered rashness of his son. "You can't go around fightin' everybody just because you haven't caught up with the man you're after."

"That's a fact, Rupe," chimed in Poke Vetter. "Take that chip off your shoulder and simmer down, son. It ain't hard to git killed in this country. You don't have to go around lookin' and askin' for it."

"All right, I'll be a good boy," Rupe said, but his tone and his smile were absent, his gray eyes far away.

Back within the boundaries of Kansas Territory, they swapped mounts for the last time and went on with their own horses toward the Osawatomie.

The flaming sunset colors were paling on the western horizon, washing into more delicate hues, when they breasted the ridge east of the farmstead. It looked good, even to Rupe's dulled eyes, the windows of the log house glowing warm and golden in the lavender-shaded grayness of twilight. The new barn and shed stood strong and secure, horses frisked in the corral, and the creek was a looping thread of silver fringed green with willows and cotton-woods. The fields stretched ripening with tall ranked corn and amber wheat and clustered vegetables, and the alfalfa meadows lay cropped and yellow. The live oaks before the house loomed somber and friendly, and small peach trees hung heavy with fruit along the stone wall. Rupe's gaze took it all in and followed his father's to the cedar-shaded rise where Jordan and his mother rested. That was the flaw in this homecoming, the pain and sorrow that kept the heart from rising in full gladness.

With dusk darkening about them they rode into the farmyard, sun-blackened, saddle-galled and silted with dust, bone-tired in the sweaty leather, their horses salt-rimed and plodding wearily. True Lambert, that squat knotty stump of a man, met them in front of the barn and shook hands with them as they swung stiffly down, asking: "Any luck?"

"Some, True," said Frank Maitland. "We settled with

Clay Hessler and Carrick and Sporn. But they had knifed Reef to death before we got there."

"And young Early?"

"We haven't seen him—yet," Rupert said.

"I'll take care of the horses," Lambert said. "You go along into the house."

Melora and Mrs. Lambert were waiting on the porch, and Melora ran out to embrace her father and Rupe, and then Poke Vetter, to his embarrassment, and Hester Lambert said, "You don't want any huggin' and kissin' from an old witch like me, but maybe you'll let me cook up somethin' for you."

Rupert bathed in the creek, where he and Jord had splashed and frolicked so often in happier days, soaping and scrubbing himself with thorough pleasure, plunging and swimming about the tiny shallow pool. Shaved and dressed in clean clothing from the skin out, he sat down at the table with Frank and Poke to do justice to the homecoming feast Hester Lambert had prepared for them.

Afterward, a cigar in his teeth, Rupe buckled on his guns, donned a short buckskin jacket, and tilted the black hat on his high tawny head. "I'm goin' into town for a while, Dad," he said. "Promised Karen I'd come and tell her—about it."

"Well, be careful, Rupe," said Frank. "Don't go rammin' around after trouble in there. It'll come quick enough."

At the corral, Rupe roped out and saddled the dun mustang, his bay having traveled far enough for one day, and loped westward along the familiar wagon road toward Trayborough. This region was peaceful now, thanks to the men who had fought and died for it, but the country at large was still torn in two by a vast Civil War, a war that clouded the entire nation and the whole future. Rupe would be in it before long. There wasn't anything else for a man of his age and temperament to do at a time like this. With Jord and Nick, he might have looked forward to the adventure of it. But alone, after having had a taste of combat in the taking of Trayborough, he saw it simply as a filthy chore that had to be done.

And reporting to Karen Hessler tonight was another unpleasant and unavoidable task. She said she had renounced her father; yet his death was bound to shock and grieve her. And Early's death, when it occurred at the hands of Rupe Maitland, would remove her finally and forever from Rupe's life. Perhaps she didn't believe so, but Rupe knew how it would be. A brother, however evil he may be, is still a brother in blood and flesh, and a woman doesn't love and marry a man who kills him, even though the brother deserves to die.

Visible for some distance, the lights of Hessler Hall bloomed over the eastern outskirts of the settlement. The picket fence lay flattened and splintered, buried here and there by debris left from the barricade. The terraced lawns, torn, trampled and gouged into raw dusty ruin, were still littered with rubble, equipment and broken magnolias. But the plantation-style house itself stood as proud and handsome as ever at the summit, and the outbuildings were clean and well-kept at the rear of the manor.

Swinging up the graveled road of the east entrance, Rupe Maitland scanned the white-pillared façade with abstract admiration for its serene dignity, and remembered with an inward pang the fateful day when he and Jord had found Karen serving drinks to Northrup, Tattam and Kivett on that gracious porch. His mind turned to the cavalry charge up that flaming slope, and he winced and shrank from the unbridled ferocity and screaming slashing horror of it. Hessler Hall was still serving as a hospital, and Rupe thought with pity of the men lying there without arms or legs, blinded, maimed and crippled for life, their future as dead as the youth they had sacrificed. Rupe thought, *Better to be like Jord and Nick Santell, dead and buried in the ground. Or Clay Hessler, a floating corpse somewhere in the Mississippi.*

And Rupe himself would have been drifting dead down the river if Dad and Poke hadn't come along in time. He thought wryly, *I didn't want to wake them up. I thought they were old and slow and I wanted to protect them. So after I bull in and botch everything up, they have to step in and save my fool neck!* It was vivid as a lightning-etched scene in his memory. He could taste the fog and gun-powder, feel the slow rain and the wet slickness of the deck, and see Clay Hessler crumpled on the rail with blood streaming down his face and Chance Carrick slumped against the glass wheelhouse, drooling darkly from his broken-toothed mouth. Then Dad, solid as a rock with that Henry leveled, and Poke Vetter, lazy, deliberate and dead-sure of himself. . . .

Rupe cantered around to the rear and stepped down at the broad stable door. Gabriel, the Negro hostler, limped out with a beaming smile. "Mistah Rupe! Ain't seen you in quite a spell. Where's that big bay geldin' of yours? You ain't lost him or nothin', I hope? He's a lot of horse."

Rupe handed him the reins. "He's fine, Gabe. You won't have to unsaddle this one. I'm not stayin' long."

Rupe Maitland walked around to the front, past the end of the porch where Asa Sporn had stood and fired the two shots wounding Rupe and killing Dodie Deneen. At the door Rupe tugged at the bell-pull, the chimes ringing their muted melody inside. A starched, immaculate colored maid came and ushered him into the vestibule. Rupe stared at the polished floor on which Nick Santell had died, and the leather settee where Dodie had lain with her dying red head on his leg.

"Miss Karen?" he inquired.

"In the library, Mistah Rupe. Follow me, if you please."

Karen, alone in the grand dim-lighted room, rose and came forward with anxious haste when she saw Rupe towering behind the maid. The colored girl withdrew, sliding the door shut after her, and Karen would have rushed into Rupe's arms if he hadn't taken her hands to forestall it. She wore a dress of soft gray material with white collar and cuffs, clinging to her firm figure to the waist and flaring out toward the floor. Her cheekbones looked slightly swollen and bruised under the powder, her dark eyes faintly discolored. He wondered at this as they studied one another.

"You went to St. Louis, Rupe?" she said quickly, as if to distract his attention from her face. "Did you—?"

"Your father's dead, Karen," he said gently. "So are Carrick and Sporn. But we didn't find Early. They killed Reef Bassett before we landed there."

None of this seemed to surprise her. Karen stared silently down at his large brown hands holding her slim white ones.

"I didn't kill your father, but I tried to," Rupe said. "I got Asa Sporn. Dad and Poke the other two."

"Did you hear anything at all about Early?"

"We heard he'd joined McCulloch's army."

"Do you—really think he has?" Karen's voice faltered strangely.

"I suppose so," Rupe said. "What happened to your face, Karen?"

She forced a laugh, freeing a hand and touching her cheek. "Oh, that? I—I was out riding, Rupe, and the horse threw me."

Rupe felt that she was lying, but he only said, "Right on your pretty face."

"It's nothing," Karen said. "Come and sit down, Rupe."

"I can't stop, Karen," said Rupert, but he permitted her to lead him to the lounge before the great unlighted fireplace. He was puzzled by the marks on her face, and something strained and unnatural in her manner. A horse-woman like Karen didn't get thrown directly on her face. She looked more as if someone had struck her open-handed, slapping back and forth across her cheeks. With Clay Hessler dead, he couldn't think of anyone who'd hit Karen—*unless it was her brother!*

"Who hit you, Karen?" he demanded suddenly.

"Hit me?" She laughed with a hint of panic. "What are you talking about, Rupert? I told you what happened."

"I don't think so, Karen," he said mildly. "But never mind. How's the hospital goin' these days?"

"We're still busy, Rupe. And some of them are still dying."

"It's a mess—and gettin' worse. It's really war now, Karen. They're fightin' in Missouri and Virginia."

Karen Hessler sighed. "I know, Rupe. You won't have to go, will you? You've fought enough right here."

"I'll be goin' pretty soon."

"Oh, Rupe! Can't you ever think of yourself and your own life—and me?"

"It's no use," Rupe said. "I'm still lookin' for Early."

Karen's gesture was desperate. "Let him go, Rupe! Can't you see it's fate? He always gets away; he never pays for anything. You believe in fate, don't you? Let Early go, forget about him, close the book on it."

Rupe's lean head shimmered with dull gold as he turned it in the soft lamplight. "I can't, Karen. It's too deep for that. I've got to get him."

Karen caught his arm and bent her shining black head against his shoulder. "I've waited so long, Rupe, and prayed so hard. Prayed that you'd come back safe, and it would be all over. Now you're here, but you won't stay and it's not ended. You won't be satisfied until you're dead, Rupe."

"Until your brother's dead, you mean," Rupert said. "You didn't act surprised about your father, Karen."

"I knew he had to die, Rupe," she murmured. "He died for me that day he shot Nick and walked out of this house."

"What did he do to Dodie?"

Karen moaned. "He—he beat her, Rupe, when she tried to fight him off. I stopped feeling like his daughter when I found out about that. Dodie was so proud and honest. He might as well have killed her. She wanted to die, Rupe. And dying to save you must have made her happy."

"I thought there was somethin' like that," Rupe Maitland said slowly, and then his voice lashed out with sudden intensity: "Now tell me who hit you, Karen! Tell me the truth! Early's back here, isn't he?"

"No, no, Rupe," she sobbed into his buckskin-clad shoulder.

"Where is he? Where's he hidin'?"

"Oh, I don't know," Karen cried despairingly. "He's gone, Rupe. He was here, trying to take me away with him. I—I wouldn't go, couldn't go—with him. He got crazy-mad and slapped me, knocked me down, even kicked me. Then he went away."

Rupe stood up, tall and straight, the bone structure of

his face standing out bleakly, straining the darkly bronzed skin. "Where? Where'd he go, Karen? He must have said somethin'."

"No, I don't know, Rupe. He just went."

"Probably gone out to shoot some more Maitlands in the back," Rupe said tautly, teeth grating on edge. "Goodbye, Karen."

She sprang up and grasped at him, pleading, "Please, Rupe! Don't go. Early's left this country for good now."

"I want to be sure of that," Rupe Maitland said, disengaging her clutching hands. "I don't want Melora and Dad shot at through the windows or bushwhacked in the barnyard." He wheeled away, trying the guns in their holsters and picking up his hat.

"Be careful, Rupert," Karen called after him, choked and brokenly. "And come back to me, Rupe, please come back!"

Rupe didn't hear her. In his mind's eye he could see Early Hessler prowling about the farmstead, waiting for a shot at his father and sister, or at Poke Vetter and the Lamberts. Rupe had to hurry now, before the last male Hessler did some more murdering.

He had to stop that sonofabitch, once and for all.

Chapter 15

The stable door was closed but for a narrow aperture, the interior lighted dimly and waveringly by a hanging lantern. Old Gabriel was nowhere in view, and nobody else was around. Rupe surveyed the moonlit shadow-patterned grounds at the rear of the mansion. Quiet except for low banjo music and plaintive singing from the Negro quarters. Rupe shoved the heavy door open far enough for the passage of a horse and stepped inside to the warm smell of horses and hay, grain and leather.

The dun mustang was in the first box stall at the right, cropping contentedly at the manger. The lantern, turned low, was suspended above the feedbox at the right of the entrance. Rupe followed his elongated shadow toward the row of stalls, alive with the munching, stomping and tail-swishing of horses. He was reaching for the gate of the stall when something stirred behind him, the whisper of boots on a hay-strewn floor. Rupe froze motionless, his eyes on the long chain looped over a peg in front of him. The mocking voice came to him then: "Don't move or you're dead, Rupe!"

Rupe's head turned for a quick glance, his stomach dropping and his spine tingling icily. Early Hessler stood there, long and limber with a gun in his right hand, the familiar scornful smile on his dark chiseled features. Handsome and elegant in gray broadcloth, a white hat rakishly cocked on his sleek black head, the other bone-handled Colt sheathed on his left thigh.

"Eyes front, Yankee," said Early Hessler. "Unbuckle your belt and let it drop. Unless you want to try reaching?"

Hands creeping with slow reluctance toward his belt buckle, Rupe Maitland estimated his chances—as if there were any. If he tried to draw he'd get a bullet in the back like Nick Santell did, and go down paralyzed and helpless with a broken spine. "Don't you Hesslers ever fight fair?" he asked wearily.

Early Hessler laughed. "You'll get your chance, Rupe. After I chop you up some. I want this to last a long time. Drop the guns and we'll have a nice little talk here."

Rupe's eyes lingered on that length of wagon chain as he fingered his belt. With his body shielding his hands from Early, there was a bare outside chance of gripping the chain and striking out with it as he turned. Little better than hopeless, but it was all Rupe had. Measuring swiftly he knew the chain would reach Hessler, and maybe in time to throw his shot off, stun and cripple him enough so Rupe could get to him—or to a gun. In these circumstances it would be better to drive straight at the man, Rupe figured. Unless Early was hurt bad, he'd be able to fire before Rupe could grab a gun off the floor, even though he lost the right-hand weapon and had to draw the left-hand gun.

"Get rid of that belt," Hessler ordered impatiently. "And turn around slow and easy, Rupe."

Rupe Maitland unlatched the buckle and let belt and guns fall with a heavy thud. Reaching for the chain with both hands, Rupe gripped and swung it like a great chattering whip as he suddenly came around with whirling speed. Early Hessler dodged and swore, his revolver exploding into the floorboards, spouting dust and splinters, as the flailing chain slashed cruelly across his right forearm and wrist, tearing the gun from his hand and dragging him off-balance in a sideways stagger.

Letting go of the chain, Rupe leaped forward at him with tigerlike fury, lashing left and right into Early's pain-twisted face, driving him backward into the baled hay by the far wall. The white hat sailed off Hessler's jerking head, and he landed flat on his shoulder blades on the hip-high bales, clawing frantically at the left holster. Blood flowed

from Early's nose and mouth and drenched the gray sleeve
on his mangled right arm.

Rupe drove in to pin him down there, but Early
brought both legs up and thrashed out with them at Rupe's
face. The bootheels caught Rupe in the upper chest and
throat with brutal choking force, kicking his head far back,
shutting off his breath, almost strangling him. Lurching
backward Rupe tripped over the stay chain and sat down
awkwardly, the jar running up his spine into his skull.

Scrambling into a sitting position on the hay bales,
Early Hessler hauled at his left-hand Colt and finally got it
out of the leather. He was just bringing it into line when
Rupe Maitland came off the floor with that chain whipping
out again, a terrible lash of linked steel smashing down
upon Hessler's left arm. The gun roared on a downward
slant, raising a fountain of hay chaff, and fell slithering on
the boards. Unarmed now and screaming in anguished rage
and hatred, Early Hessler snatched a broad-tined pitchfork
off the wall and lunged forward off the bales in a headlong
charge, the sharp-pointed fork held spearlike before him.

Rupe backed away, gasping and sobbing for air, and as
Early closed in for the murderous thrust, Rupe slammed
the near end of the chain across his pumping legs. Hessler
hurled the fork as he went down, tripped and shackled by
the biting steel links that wound his ankles. Rupe ducked
low, feeling the breeze of the two-tined hayfork as it
whipped overhead and stuck quivering and twanging in the
wooden side of the grainbox.

Early Hessler was kicking frenziedly free of the chain,
when Rupe reached him with ripping rights and lefts that
spattered scarlet spray and knocked Early flat and sliding
on the back of his neck, boots high in the air. Rebounding
from the baled hay, Early swiveled about on all fours and
launched himself at Rupe's knees in a low flying tackle.
They went down in a rolling tangled welter, striking with
fist and elbow, knee and boot, as they thrashed about in the
stifling stable dust, first one on top and then the other.

Sprung apart by mutual violence and weariness floundering away from one another on hands and knees, Early
Hessler found Rupe's gun belt directly in front of him. With

a bloody gloating snarl, Early raked out the Remington, and reared about to locate his target. But Rupe Maitland was up through some superhuman effort, up and driving straight at the kneeling Hessler, crashing full tilt into him and over him, kicking the gun clear into the corner by the feedbox and stumbling on after it.

Groaning and retching, Early Hessler rolled over onto all fours again, his arms torn and bruised by that chain, his face a horrible misshapen mask of crimson, and pawed half-blind for the holstered Colt. He yanked it out and hammered a shot after Rupe, but Rupe was bending low for Jord's .44 Remington and the slug seared past his bowed blond head and splintered the grainbox, near the pitchfork.

Gun in hand and cocked, Rupe Maitland swung around in a widespread crouch, thumbing the hammer forward as the barrel swerved into line, the Remington roaring flame and leaping up in Rupe's hand. The kneeling Hessler rocked back, haunches on heels, bloody gun hand drooping, the Colt blasting a furrow in the floor, raising dirty streamers of splintered wood. Rupe leveled off and fired once more, Jord's old gun flaring and springing hard, as Early Hessler shuddered, blowing blood as he toppled backward, squirmed over onto his stomach and lay still at last, his face against the dusty floorboards.

Rupe stood for a minute staring down at the silent figure, aware for the first time of the panicked horses plunging and whickering in their stalls. "Thank God—it's done," Rupe panted slowly, thrusting the gun into his waistband. Turning to the water trough, he ducked his sweaty head and grimed face, washing his blackened raw-knuckled hands. When he straightened, dripping, Karen was there by the door and Doc Kinderness was stooped beside Early's body.

"I didn't know, Rupe," said Karen. "I didn't know he was out here."

"I didn't hardly think you'd sent me out here to die," Rupe said. "I'm sorry, Karen—but it had to be done."

"Yes, I know it did, Rupert. And I want you to know this, Rupe: I lost my father and my brother—before they ever died."

"Well, it's over, Karen," said Rupe. "That's all I'm really glad about—havin' it finished." He walked toward the dun's stall.

Doc Kinderness straightened and looked gravely at him. "The end of the feud, Rupe? Are you hurt, son?" He draped a blanket over Early.

"No, Doc. Just mussed up a little."

Karen Hessler came and plucked shyly at his buckskin sleeve. "Where are you going now, Rupert?"

"Home, first. And then the army."

She lifted her dark head and pure profile. "I'm going with you, Rupe, because that's where I belong. Whether you believe it or not. I can't let you go—like this."

"No, Karen." Rupe shook his wet bronze head. "There's no future in it, for us."

"There's tonight, there's *now*, Rupert. Tonight, tomorrow, a few more days perhaps. That's better than nothing, Rupe. That's enough—for me."

Rupe looked uncertainly at her, then at the floor, his gray eyes tired and troubled. "I don't know, Karen—"

"I can't stay here, Rupe. I've got to go with you."

"She's right, Rupe," said Doc Kinderness solemnly. "As they wrote in the ancient Sanskrit, '*Look to this day, for it is life.*' You two have wasted enough time. In a world like this, you can't afford to waste any more. Take her outside, Rupe, and I'll saddle another horse.

The stable yard was deep in shadow-traced moonlight and stillness, the Negro music having ceased, and the night air washed clean and cool on their bare heads and fevered faces. They stood in silence for an interval, watching the moonbeams gild the rooftops with silver, listening to the muted sounds of the hospital and the town below, the small night life in the fields and trees.

"Are you sure, Karen, you know what you're doin'?" Rupe Maitland asked somberly, at last.

"Yes, I know," Karen Hessler said softly, and then she smiled up at him with a rare flash of spirit and courage and humor, pitting her woman's will and love against all the adversity and heartbreak in a merciless world.

"My father told me to stay with my damned Yankee. The best advice he ever gave me. And that's just what I'm going to do, Rupert. As long as he wants me."

"That's a life sentence, lady," said Rupert Maitland, with a grave tender smile.

ABOUT THE AUTHOR

ROE RICHMOND is an old-time author of Westerns who ranks with Luke Short and Ernest Haycox for the authenticity and action of his fiction. A Vermont native, Mr. Richmond graduated from the University of Michigan and, before turning to writing full time, he worked as a ranch hand out West and played semiprofessional baseball. He and his wife Evelyn raised a son during the bleakest years of the Depression while the author wrote award-winning short stories and books. Having penned more than twenty novels of the West, Mr. Richmond retired from writing and currently lives in Concord, New Hampshire.

WESTERNS THAT DON'T BACK DOWN

ROE RICHMOND is one of that rare breed of Western writers whose novels of adventure continue to grip generation after generation of readers. An award winning storyteller of power and passion, he brings the authentic old West vividly back to life.

BRIAN GARFIELD is one of the best-selling Western Writers of his generation. He mined the rich motherlode of frontier history to create powerful novels of hard-edged men and the unforgiving land in which they lived. Garfield stands tall among the finest writers of frontier fiction.

Wherever Bantam Books are sold or use this handy coupon:

Elmore Leonard "should be a household name."
—*The Philadelphia Inquirer*

His characters become etched in your mind, his dialogue snaps off the page, and his keen understanding of the violent tensions between people who live on the edge will rivet you to your chair. Bantam offers you these exciting titles:

And if Western adventure is what you're after, Bantam has these tales of the frontier to offer from ELMER KELTON, one of the great Western storytellers with a special talent for capturing the fiercely independent spirit of the West: